PUBLISHABLE BY DEATH

ACF Bookens

VINCI BOOKS

By ACF Bookens

St. Marin's Cozy Mystery Series

Publishable By Death

Entitled To Kill

Bound To Execute

Plotted For Murder

Tome To Tomb

Scripted To Slay

Proof Of Death

Epilogue Of An Epitaph

Hardcover Homicide

Picture Book Peril

Dog-Eared Danger

For Mom,
who taught me to read and modeled the joy of disappearing into story.

Vinci Books

vinci-books.com

Published by Vinci Books Ltd in 2025

1

Printed and bound in Great Britain by Clays Ltd, Elcograf S.p.A.

Chapter One

It was a brisk March morning as I walked away from the cove toward Main Street in St. Marin's, Maryland. In the shadow of the buildings, I was just beginning to see the tops of daffodils poking up their heads, but today, I tugged the hood of my long sweater up higher on my head and pulled the collar of my peacoat closed. Short hair was perfect for the warmer days – and for owning my ever-graying locks – but in these cold months, I sometimes missed my long ponytail. Spring was coming, but it didn't feel much like it today. We'd had ice overnight, and while the temperature had gone above freezing already, the roads were still wet and ice clung to the edge of puddles.

Still, I practically skipped down the sidewalk, even though skipping isn't always that flattering on a slightly plump forty-four-year-old. I didn't care. This was going to be the first weekend my new bookstore was open.

I slid my key into the lock on the front door of the old gas station and put a little muscle into turning it in the glass-fronted door. As I swung it open, I took a minute to enjoy the little bell above my head as it chimed. That bell had been hanging over that door as long as anyone in town could remember, so every long-time resident of St. Marin's told me when they stopped by to say hi and take a gander at the newest shop in their — I mean, *our* quaint town. I loved that bell, not just because it was part of the charm of this building, but because I looked forward to hearing it when it meant people were visiting *my* bookshop.

I had just come back to St. Marin's the previous October. I visited when I was a kid on a summer trip from our family home over near Baltimore, and I'd never forgotten the charm and friendliness of this waterside community.

I hadn't had much time to socialize since coming back though. I'd hit the ground running because I wanted the shop open as soon as possible. I needed the income to help build my book inventory, but also to be able to help pay the mortgage. My best friend Mart — an expert on wineries — was helping cover the bills for our house since she had a good paying job at a local up-and-coming winery nearby and was consulting all over the East Coast. I felt kind of bad living off of Mart's generosity, especially since she had basically followed me here from the West Coast when I'd decided to live my dreams and open a bookstore back here on the Eastern Shore of Maryland, but I knew that Mart didn't mind and that I'd pay my friend back in time.

Today, though, I needed to finish painting the brick walls at the front of the store. I loved the charm of the old red bricks that I figured had probably been made nearby, but years of smokers and exhaust had made them dingy and smelly . . . so a good white-washing helped spiff them up and made the shop look cozy instead of dirty. I wanted the place to recall the old gas station that it originally was, just not too much.

I had to get the window displays ready, too. In the north window that had once been the station office, I was putting up a collection of books about Harriet Tubman, the woman St. Marin's was honoring this weekend in their annual Harriet Tubman Festival. Tubman had been enslaved just down the road a piece, and this annual festival honored her memory and her work on the Underground Railroad while also trying to educate people about the history and continuing legacy of slavery. Local historians and genealogists were going to be giving talks all over town, and I was hoping that Catherine Clinton, the woman who wrote my favorite book on Tubman, might come by and sign the copies of her book for the shop since she was in town for a presentation at the local library.

In the other window, which had opened onto the actual garage section of the gas station, I wanted to put out some of my favorite gardening books, including titles that ranged from how to build and maintain a raised-bed vegetable garden to how to start a cut flower business. I'd asked around about what kind of gardeners were in the community and quickly found out that St. Mariners were passionate about their plants. I took that intel to heart and stocked books in a sizable garden section near the rear of the store, where I had also placed a wingback chair upholstered in floral fabric, one of my favorite antique store finds.

The rest of the store was equally cozy with big armchairs, lots of tables where readers could set a mug of something warm, and dog beds positioned strategically to accommodate any pup, but especially Mayhem, my new rescue puppy. Mayhem had been named Maxine at the shelter, and I had picked her because she was – it seemed – the calmest in the litter. As soon as I got her home, though, the little gal had started chewing anything wooden that she could find – a beautiful piece of driftwood I had picked up on Bodega Beach, one of the wine barrel staves that Mart had brought home to use for a sign by our house, even the table leg of the farm table we had purchased at a yard sale back in November. Plus, Aslan, my cat, took immediately to hiding under my bed anytime the puppy was nearby because the dog desperately wanted to be her friend. I had started calling her Mayhem as a joke, and the name stuck.

Fortunately, the Black Mouth Cur – a friend on Facebook had told me that was Mayhem's breed after seeing a picture – had no affinity for chewing books. She was already a fixture at the shop, often taking up residence in a sunbeam coming through the north window while I worked. If nothing else, her presence was sure to bring business if the number of people who stopped to talk to her through the glass was an indication.

Today, I had left her home to rest up. I hoped tomorrow's shop traffic would be heavy, and Mayhem insisted on greeting everyone who came in. The puppy needed to conserve her energy.

Once, on a trip to visit a friend in Denver, I had visited a bookstore in Frisco, Colorado, and had loved that the owner's Bernese Mountain Dog had free rein of the shop. I had vowed then and there that I'd have an open door policy for pooches if I ever was able to fulfill my dream of owning my own bookstore.

My own bookstore. I stopped mid-paint stroke and let out a long heavy breath. I'd done it. I'd finally done it. Tomorrow, I was opening my own bookstore. I shivered a little with excitement.

The bell rang over the door, and in came Woody Isherwood, the town woodworker. Woody was a white man about seventy, short and stout like a teapot, and I imagined he had been able to lift most anything back in the day.

I had come to know him when Mayhem had gotten her teeth into an antique table at one of the local store's sidewalk sales and I had needed to buy the table and then have it repaired. Woody had done a splendid job of turning the small console table into a cute little stool that was perfect for that garden section wing chair. So, when I decided I wanted a wood-burned sign for the shop, I'd contacted Woody first thing.

Now, here he was, ready to hang his creation. The sign was made from several planks of reclaimed wood that Woody got from an old tobacco barn down the road, and the shop name – All Booked Up – was burned deep into the gray wood. It was the perfect blend of rustic and nautical, and I thought it was one of the most beautiful things I'd ever seen.

"Woody, thank you so much. I can't wait to see it up there."

"You're most welcome, Harvey. But before I hang it, I have a question for you."

"Sure." I sat down on the edge of the platform I'd built by the south window for future readings by local and visiting authors. "What's your question?"

Woody looked a little sheepish behind his silver beard, but he looked me in the eye and said, "Your given name Harvey?"

I smiled. I got this question a lot, especially from the old-timers over here in the rural Eastern Shore. One old fellow had even gone so far as to say, "That's a man's name. Your folks must've wanted a boy."

"My name is Anastasia Lovejoy Beckett. At least that's what my birth certificate says, but I never felt much like an Anastasia, and Lovejoy is what everyone called my granny. So somewhere along the way, my dad just started calling me Harvey, and it stuck."

Woody grinned. "I could call you Stacy if you'd like to go back to your roots."

"No thank you," I nearly shouted. "Harvey is just fine."

Woody laughed and then glanced out the window. "Ah, there's my assistant for the day."

I stood up and saw a thin, dark-haired, white man in coveralls coming to the door. I ran a hand through my short, graying hair and was embarrassed to find it coated in a thin layer of paint splatter. *You can't take me anywhere.*

The door chimed, and the man walked in. Woody nodded at the man. "Harvey Beckett, I expect you know Daniel Galena from the garage up the street."

"Nice to meet you, Harvey."

I took a step forward and used the second to catch my breath. This man was super handsome in a down-home kind of way, and he had a dimple in his right cheek. I never had been able to resist a dimple. "Ah, you're the infamous St. Marin's mechanic." I put out my hand. "Nice to meet you."

His smile grew. "And you're the brave woman who has decided our decrepit gas station needs new life."

I felt the color rise to my cheeks. "It's a beautiful building. I'm honored to fill it again. Do you read?"

This time, Daniel blushed. "Oh no, ma'am. I mean I love books, but I'm not much of a reader myself. More hands-on." He held his hands out in front of him, and I noticed that they were calloused and a bit dirty. It was endearing.

5

"Ah, well, we're not all book people in this world. For my part, I have trouble finding the thingy that releases my hood, and the best description of a car I can give is its color. I drive a blue car, for the record."

"A midnight blue 2012 Subaru Outback," he said without hesitation.

"You've seen my car."

He grinned. "It's a small town, and I know cars."

Woody cleared his throat, and I realized that I'd kind of been flirting. The woodsmith gave me a wink and said, "You ready to help the lady with this sign?"

"Yes sir. Let's get this up so that it's ready for grand opening. Tomorrow, right?"

"Yep. I hope you'll both come. We'll have food and The Watermen – the band not the actual fishermen – are going to play. It'll be a fun night."

"The Mrs. and I will be here. I hear it's alright if we bring along Missy."

"Of course. Children are always welcome."

Woody let out a roar of a laugh. "Oh Missy's our Chesapeake Bay Retriever."

I blushed and smiled. "Well, still true. Definitely bring Missy. Mayhem will be here. We're a dog-friendly shop."

"In that case," Daniel said, "Maybe I'll bring Taco."

I felt my smile grow wider. "Not your son, I take it."

It was Daniel's turn to laugh. "I don't have any kids, and I certainly hope I wouldn't name one of them Taco. No, he's my Basset Hound."

"I love Basset Hounds." As if this guy wasn't already catching my eye, he was the owner of one of my favorite breeds. I was probably doomed.

Woody opened the door, and the bell rang again. "We'll get this up in a jiffy, Harvey. See you tomorrow."

I had been excited before, but now, people were really coming. Dogs, too. And Daniel, well, that might just be a little bonus.

Chapter Two

When I woke at six, Mart was already up and making breakfast. Even at this early hour and after a wild week at work, she looked like she'd just stepped out of a J. Jill catalog with her messy pony tail and rosy cheeks. On some people, this kind of natural beauty – dark hair not yet graying and clear, glowing skin – might make me a little jealous, but on my best friend, it just fit the kindness of her spirit. "You can't go to your grand opening on an empty stomach. Bacon, eggs, and some of those scones from that little patisserie over in Annapolis. You sit. I'll bring it over."

I wiped the sleep from my eyes and tried not to trip over Mayhem – who had strategically positioned herself below the bacon pan – as I made my way to the table. I noted that Aslan had wisely found a perch on top of the bookshelf in the dining room. She too hoped for bacon, but she knew it best not to try the dog's overzealous attempts at friendship when fried pork was involved.

As I perched on a bar stool, I said, "You didn't have to do this. You've already done so much."

"Oh please. It's the grand opening of the bookstore that we've been working hard to open for five months now. It's the least I can do. You saved me from the uppity world of northern California wineries and brought me to this place where the very little bit I know about wine seems like I invented the stuff. I'm a valuable commodity over here, and I like it." She tossed her hair like she was walking the runway and returned to the stovetop.

Mart was trying to make light of the notoriety she'd already gained as an expert in wine operations. She was the head of marketing at the local winery, but as soon as she'd arrived, other wineries had asked for her help in promoting their places. Fortunately, she was able to do both because she loved the local spot but also thrived on the travel and time with people. She was every bit the extrovert to my introvert self.

This weekend, she'd turned down a really impressive – and well-paying opportunity – near Charlottesville, Virginia to consult with a celebrity winery owner just so she could be here for my grand opening. I was very grateful because I wasn't sure I could do this without her, but I still felt a little guilty.

Mart set a huge plate of food in front of me and then placed a small saucer of eggs up on the bookshelf for Aslan. My best friend had been totally suckered into believing that poor cat was suffering, and that chubby feline was not going to dissuade her of that delusion.

I looked down at Mayhem. She was sitting up, head on my thigh, hopeful. She knew the bacon was an unlikely treat, but maybe some of those eggs would make their way to her waiting mouth. I gave her a scratch and then tucked into the food.

By seven, Mayhem, Mart, and I were walking up to the shop. Woody's sign looked great, the strings of Edison bulbs that I'd splurged on were giving the front windows a warm glow, and the bright pink Grand Opening banner on the awning at the front of the store was shining bright in the glow of the morning moonlight.

I had a lot riding on today in terms of money, but also reputation. If the store didn't get a good start, it would be hard for me to gain enough momentum to stay up, much less grow. So I'd gone all in. I'd taken out ads in the local newspaper, posted to Facebook in every book-related group in the area, and pushed out a huge press release about the grand opening. The local paper, the *St. Marin's*

Courier, had come out to interview me for a feature piece in last Sunday's edition.

The reporter, Lucia Stevensmith, had visited the shop last Thursday for an interview, and I had been so excited that she wanted to be in the space and get a feel of it. But I almost immediately regretted that we hadn't gone down to the waterfront or something. The look on her face when she walked in wasn't a welcome, excited one. She looked like she'd just tasted a raw persimmon for the first time. Her thin face was puckered, and beneath her graying eyebrows, her eyes were tiny with what I thought was disgust. "Oh, I see you haven't gone for a full remodel," was the first thing she said.

Then, she was bossy to the extreme and gave me advice about how to organize the shelves, suggested I move the location of the register closer to the door for "loss prevention" – it took me forever to figure out she meant shoplifting – and tried to persuade me that I'd never be successful with a general bookstore. "You need to specialize in something. Maybe nautical books or history about Maryland. You're just not going to find people who want to read mystery novels AND buy nature guides."

"I read mystery novels and buy nature guides. I'm sure I'm not the only one," I had said.

She had let a little snort out and continued her critique as she moved into our small café. Apparently, I would "lose my shirt" with food. "Total money pit." I had found it hard not to either defend myself or cry, but I silently bore up under her barrage.

Finally, Mart had put a stop to her bevy of "suggestions" by saying that she had prepared cappuccinos for us. "Is it decaf? I don't touch anything but decaf after ten a.m. I have a sensitive system," she'd said. Mart told her that it was not decaf, and I was pretty sure Stevensmith whispered the word "heathens" under her breath, but decided to let it go.

The interview itself was pretty straightforward, and I was grateful for the chance to talk about my hopes for the shop – that people would make it a place they gathered, that they'd suggest titles I should carry and authors they'd like to see read here, and that All

Booked Up would become a part of St. Marin's, just like the other wonderful shops on Main Street.

Stevensmith had said, "How quaint" with a certain dismissive tone and then snapped a few pictures with her phone before heading out. Fortunately, the paper had sent over a photographer the next day, and they had done a nice piece with a few great photos and key quotes in the Sunday edition. Most of Stevensmith's persnicketiness had gotten edited out, thank goodness.

When I'd asked Woody about the reporter, he'd rolled his eyes. "That woman rubs every single human on the earth the wrong way. She always has an opinion about everything, and is never afraid to share it. In fact, just last week, she started telling Lucas – the director of the maritime museum – that she thought they should get rid of the exhibition about the enslaved men who fished these waters and ran boats along the waterways here because it made people uncomfortable." I knew I liked Lucas immediately when Woody said the director had rolled his eyes and said, "That's sort of the point, Lucia."

"Well, I'm glad it's not just me, then?" I asked Woody.

"Nope, pretty much nobody likes the woman, but we try to be neighborly, you know."

I did know. In small southern communities, neighborliness was the currency on which everyone survived. Without each other, no one would make it. But of course, this also meant there were a fair number of crotchety folks that people had to put up with, and apparently, I'd met one. Lucky me.

When we arrived at the store, I unlocked the shop door, smiling as the bell rang above me, and held it open for Mart as she headed right to the register with most of my savings in small bills to make change.

I walked to the back of the store and turned on a second bank of lights by the art and gardening books. I'd wait a bit before I turned on everything since I wasn't quite ready for customers yet.

Opening time for this first day was eight a.m. since I'd promised fresh baked goods, hot coffee, and plenty of hot cocoa in the café. I expected my only employee – Raquel – to be in shortly to staff the food and beverage side of things.

Rocky, as she preferred to be called, was a tender but confident young woman of about twenty. She took classes at Salisbury, a local university, but still lived at home. Each time I'd met with her to plan the café, her hair had been done in another stylish look – once she had long braids, once a wild pixy cut that framed her face and set off her light-brown skin perfectly. Someday, I'd get up the nerve to get tips on hairstyles from her. But today, I had just managed to get a little pomade in to tame my curls in the short cut I've gotten from the salon up the street. The last thing I needed was to worry about a bad hair day.

While I fussed with the books a bit more, Mart made sure the register was stocked and the tablet that we'd use to take credit cards was working. Then, she began laying small piles of postcards with the shop hours, events, and contact information on all the tables. If she didn't already have a job (and if I had the money), I'd be looking to hire her as my marketing advisor. She was *so good* at this stuff.

The bell chimed, and Rocky came in with her arms full of what looked to be cinnamon rolls doused in icing. Despite my full breakfast, my mouth started watering. "What are those?" Mart asked, coming over to help Rocky carry everything.

"My mom makes the best cinnamon rolls. She whipped up a batch this morning for the grand opening."

I gently peeled back the plastic wrap and leaned down to take a long, slow inhale. "Is that maple icing?"

"Sure is. Mom's specialty."

"I'll be having one of those later," I said, "and maybe if we get good traffic today, we could ask your mom if she'd make these for us regularly." This weekend would bring the biggest off-seasons crowds for the Tubman festival, so I sure hoped it meant we'd get some good traffic, too.

"I expect she could be persuaded," Rocky said as she pushed

back the stray strand of black hair that had slipped forward from her gorgeous halo of curls. "I'll get everything set up."

The café was small, just three or four tables in what used to be the garage bay of the gas station, a counter, a baked goods case, and an espresso machine, but I hoped it would encourage customers to stay a while. St. Marin's didn't have a formal coffee shop, so I wanted this to be a place people would hang out, do a little work, maybe read a book and make a purchase, too.

At the back of the garage bay behind the café, Woody and a friend had built a wall and created a storeroom for me. Right now, it was mostly empty since I couldn't afford to have much inventory that wasn't already on the floor, but I looked forward to seeing boxes of books, especially for author events and holiday sales, filling the space.

I took a quick look around the shop to be sure everything was good and then headed to the back to get a few more of the paper bags Mart had bought for the grand opening. They each had our shop name and a sketch of the storefront printed on them, and I wanted to be certain Rocky had some for the café in case anyone wanted to take a pastry for the road.

I stepped into the back room and flipped on the light. Then, I screamed.

There, on the floor, was the body of a woman. She was sprawled out like whatever had killed her had taken her by surprise, and while I didn't see any blood, I was sure she was dead. There's just something about a living person's body – a movement even when that person is still – that a dead body doesn't have. This was my second time finding someone dead, and I didn't love that now I'd have two images of lifeless bodies haunting me.

Mart and Rocky came running and stopped short as soon as they could see over my shoulders. "Oh my word," Rocky said.

I took a deep breath and reached for my phone just as Mart said, "Isn't that the reporter who was here the other day? The rude woman?"

With a few more steps, I was at the body. I leaned down, and sure enough, it was Lucia Stevensmith. "Maybe we shouldn't call her rude anymore," I said to Mart. I was trying to lighten the mood, but really I just wanted to cry. Someone had died in my store on my opening day.

Within minutes, Sheriff Mason had arrived with a new deputy named Williams. The sheriff was beloved in St. Marin's because he was absolutely no-nonsense when it came to police work, but also super funny. When the high school football team had won the State Championships back in November, the sheriff had organized the townspeople to line the road into St. Marin's with scarecrows holding each players' names, and when they reached the town square, there was a huge banner that said, "Catamounts are no scaredy cats" hanging in front of a huge, stuffed mountain lion pinning down a tiny "rebel" soldier that represented the mascot of the team they'd just beaten. Mart had said that was very "on brand" since the African American sheriff was also known for "having a conversation" with anyone who thought it fitting to hang a Confederate flag in his town. "Maybe it is heritage, but it's a heritage of hate," he'd said in a local newspaper. I pretty much loved him for that.

When he and Officer Williams, a petite, almost tiny, black woman who looked like her utility belt might drag her to the ground at any moment, showed up in the back room of my store, I let out the breath I hadn't even been aware I was holding. The sheriff took a very close look at Stevensmith's body and then escorted us out of the room before saying, "Probably not the opening day attention you were hoping for, huh, Harvey?" He gave me a wry grin and then dispatched Williams to call the coroner before guiding me to the café to get my statement.

"You okay?" he asked as we sat down.

I nodded, grateful for his kindness. He'd been by a few times, just to say hello and let us know his staff was keeping an eye on things as we got the shop started. I had appreciated his attention and already felt like he was a friend.

"Okay, so just tell me what you know." His voice was soft and encouraging.

"Not much to tell," I began. "I went in the back room, and there she was." I told him about my morning, about when I arrived, in as much detail as I could remember, hoping that something would help.

Mason nodded and made a few notes. Then he sat back, took a long sip of his cappuccino with extra foam, and said, "One of the things we'll have to figure out is how she got in. I know there's a back door off the garage, I mean café, right? I expect you keep that locked."

I nodded. "Of course." I tried to remember closing up the night before, but I had been so tired that I only remembered getting home, eating cereal for dinner, and collapsing into bed. "But it's been a busy few days. Let me check."

I walked back past the storeroom, the sheriff close behind, to the half-glass back door that opened onto a small parking lot and turned the handle. It opened right up. "Oh no! I must have forgotten to lock it."

The sheriff stepped around me and looked closely at the door jamb. "Nope, looks like someone credit carded it."

"That's actually a thing people can do? I thought it was just on TV shows."

"Actually a thing. Pretty easy, too, on a door like this at least." He turned to the storeroom door. "Let me show you." The sheriff took a grocery store discount club card out of his wallet, turned the simple tab on the storeroom doorknob, and pulled the door shut. Then, he took the card, slid it between the door and the jamb, and worked it down until he was at the latch. Then, he wiggled the card a bit, and the door popped open. "See. Pretty easy."

"Glory! Alright, I'm having a deadbolt put on that backdoor right away."

"Good plan. I'll ask Williams to check for prints – not that it's likely we'll get much that's usable – and then you can call your alarm company. I might go with a full-on security bar if I were you. It would keep the door locked but also let you know if someone tried to sneak out of the store from the back. Should be easy to do before the end of the day."

"Thanks." I looked at my watch – 7:45. I was supposed to open in fifteen minutes. I let out a long sigh of disappointment.

Mason looked at me and smiled. "Don't worry, Harvey. It'll only take the coroner a minute to load out Stevensmith's body, and then no one will be the wiser. After all, she was our only reporter. No one left to tell the story." He winked.

I laughed hesitantly. "Some people might think you're a little flippant about a death, Sheriff."

He frowned. "Never. But then, it's not going to bring her back for me to be overly serious is it." A smile crept into the corner of his mouth. "Besides, we don't want to hurt business in our newest shop here in town. I'll do my best to keep this quiet until this afternoon."

"Oh, thank you, Sheriff. I mean, I don't want to hinder an investigation or anything, but if there's no harm in keeping things quiet . . ."

"Actually, it might be a help. As soon as word gets out, everyone will have a theory. This will give me a few hours to get a handle on things before the entire town starts in on my cellphone." He tapped the smartphone holstered opposite his pistol. "Now, how about another of those cinnamon rolls while we wait?"

Chapter Three

By the time we closed the shop at seven p.m. that first day, I was some dazzling combination of exhausted and exhilarated that had me smiling nonstop, but also very much in need of a comfy chair and an ottoman. Mart locked the front door, and I collapsed in the chair-and-a-half by the fiction section, curling my feet up under me and dropping my head back on the overstuffed cushion.

"That was A.MA.ZING." Mart said as she slumped to the floor against the bookshelf next to me. "There must have been 1,000 people through here today."

"1,312 to be exact."

"You were counting?!"

I held up the silver counter-clicker I'd picked up at an office supply store when I'd visited Salisbury last week. "I come prepared."

"Love it! So over 1,300 people. Wow. No wonder we're so tired."

"Tired doesn't even begin to cover it. I still can't believe I have my own bookstore."

"Not only that, but Catherine Clinton signed her books AND agreed to come do a book event for you in April. That's huge."

"It is . . . but not as huge as finding a dead body in my back room." I was so excited that Clinton was coming to sign, but all day,

I'd kept flashing back to the image of Lucia Stevensmith's lifeless body. It had been a great grand opening day . . . but a tainted one. I hadn't liked the reporter, but I was still sad that she had died – and horrified that someone had killed her, killed her in my shop.

Mart sighed. "Right."

The sheriff had come by late in the day to say the coroner had ruled the cause of death to be a blow to the head by something cylindrical.

"The reporter in the storeroom with a candlestick," Sheriff Mason had said with a terrible English accent, and I hadn't been able to keep from laughing. I sounded a little hysterical to myself. The fatigue and double-adrenaline shot of the grand opening and the murder had started to fray my nerves.

"I don't think there's anything shaped like that in my store," I said, looking around and finding myself grateful that the sheriff had come by in jeans and a "Meyerhoff's Grocery" T-shirt instead of his uniform.

"Doesn't look like she was hit here."

"Oh, thank God," I said a little too loudly as several shoppers turned to look. "I mean, the woman is still dead, and that's still horrible. But I didn't like thinking she'd died here."

"Well, I didn't say that." The sheriff looked a little sheepish as I gave him a squinty look. "I said she wasn't hit here. But it does look like she stumbled in here, maybe to hide."

I puffed up my cheeks. "Would she have been able to credit card my door with a head injury like that?"

"Human beings are capable of a great many things when driven by necessity. I'm not sure that's what happened, but it seems likely. We found Stevensmith's fingerprints on the outside of the door."

I nodded and lowered my voice. "Okay, so she did die here. I suppose in a few years we might be able to trot out her ghost for a spooky book night." I immediately winced as the words left my mouth. "Too soon?"

"Nope. You're thinking like a business woman, and I like it. Plus, the ghost tours around here are pretty epic."

I laughed. I loved when older people like me used slang, especially when it was a little behind the times. "I'll make a note."

From her now-reclining position on the floor, Mart said, "Did the sheriff have any leads on the murder?"

"Not that he told me." In fact, he'd as much as told me to stop asking questions when I'd asked. "He was pretty tight-lipped. But I have some theories."

Mart sat up. "Ooh, I love a good theory. Tell me."

"Well," I said, resting my elbows on my knees, "It's not like Stevensmith was everybody's favorite person. Did you meet Ms. Heron when she came in today? White woman about my height. Blonde hair to her chin. Mud on her shirt."

"Oh yes, I remember her. I wondered about the mud."

"She grows her flowers and veggies and then sells them at that little farm stand at the end of the street. She'd been planting potatoes all day. Hence the dirt."

Mart nodded. "Got it. What about her?"

"She stopped by earlier in the week to see if I wanted to buy any flowers for the café tables when they were ready. She'd seen Stevensmith's article and wanted to show her support, one business woman to another. While she was here, she told me that Stevensmith had slammed her stand when it first opened." I tried my best imitation of Heron's thick, Eastern Maryland accent, "She said my carrots were dirty and my zinnias 'limpid.' I wanted to kill the woman."

"Ooh, and then, there she is dead." Mart's eyes were wide, and I could see the wheels of suspicion turning.

"Exactly. I don't think Eleanor would do that, but it was interesting. Sheriff said there wasn't much love lost for the old reporter. Kind of makes me feel bad for the woman – I mean I feel bad she's dead – but, well, she was a pretty serious pain in the tuchus."

"That's putting it mildly." Mart lay back down on the floor and stared at the ceiling. "But let's talk about the important stuff. That mechanic and his pup were sure cute."

Mayhem, who had been snoring away on her dog bed by the cash register, sat up at the mention of Taco. They'd taken an immediate liking to each other. Mart laughed, "Like owner like dog.

I tried to act cool by draping my legs over one end of the chair and lacing my fingers behind my head, but Mart was on to me. "Oh my gracious. You like him!" She sat up. "You like him a lot!"

I knew my face was as red as the spine on the Everyman's Library edition of *Love in the Time of Cholera*. There was no hiding it. I had a crush.

Daniel had come in around lunch with Taco on a leash. The dog walked into the store like he'd been visiting bookshops all his life. Daniel unhooked him, and the Basset walked to the dog bed by the animal section and climbed in, stretching his full length so his head draped onto the floor. "He does know how to make himself comfortable," I said.

"Yes, he does. He's never met a bed he didn't like." Daniel was grinning with pride.

I smiled. "Glad you guys could come."

"Wouldn't have missed it." He smiled back.

Just remembering his visit brought my grin right back. "And you know what, Mart?" I gave up all pretense of nonchalance. "He bought a copy of *Possession* because I recommended it."

"You recommended that a mechanic who doesn't really read buy a book about two English academics who fall in love?"

"I did." I had felt kind of proud of myself for the brazenness, but was quickly deflated by Mart's practicality.

"What if he hates it?"

I sighed. *Oh no, what if he did?*

Before my mind could slide off into worst-case scenarios, Mart reminded me another odd happening from the day. "Who was that young guy, the one with the skateboard and the hair a la Fresh Prince?"

I knew just who she was talking about. A young black man – maybe about twenty – had come in and asked if we had a restroom.

I'd pointed him to the back of the store then didn't think anything of it until a while later when he came by the counter again. "You're out of paper towels," he said.

"Oh no. I'll take care of that right away," I said as I turned to go to the cabinet where we kept supplies by the bathrooms "Thanks for telling me."

"Least I could do since I used the last two rolls."

I stopped my jog to the storeroom just as Mart came up to the counter. I turned back to the customer. "Are you okay? Were you sick or something? I can get you a ginger ale."

He shrugged. "Oh no, I'm fine. Sorry for using all your paper towels." He waved and then headed back out to the street with his skateboard.

Mart and I watched him cross the street and head off further into town. But then, a customer came up to ask about wine books, and Mart was off in her element. And I rushed to refill the paper towels in the men's room.

Standing up from the chair and stretching, I said, "Yeah, that was odd. But the bathroom was immaculate after he was in there. I just hope he was okay."

Mart pried herself off the floor. "Guess we can head home? Unless you just want to sleep here to save us the trouble." I was tempted, but Aslan would have my hide if I didn't come home to feed her and tend her, er, facilities. She was a very particular cat.

The next day, the shop was hopping again. News of Stevensmith's murder was in the Sunday paper, and that, coupled with the great coverage that the *Baltimore Sun* had done about the shop meant we were even more crowded than we'd been the day before. A couple of visitors even asked if they could see "where it happened," and I had to politely decline the prurient requests, including one from Max Davies, the owner of Chez Cuisine, the local pseudo-French restaurant.

"Too bad," Davies said. "I kind of wanted to revel in the place of her death."

I must not have been good at hiding my look of horror because he said, "Oh, come on. I know you met her. She wasn't the most likeable person after all."

"Well, no," I had to admit, "but the woman was murdered. Maybe reveling isn't the kindest reaction?"

"If she had tried to shut down your business, you might feel differently."

"She tried to shut you down?"

"Hm-mm. Twice. Once when she wrote a scathing review of our escargot and called them, 'Elasticine.' My snails are fresh and succulent, I'll have you know."

I nodded vigorously because it seemed like it was in my best interest to stay on Davies' good side.

"The second time, I know she was behind this trumped-up health department complaint. I've never had rats in my kitchen." He sniffed as if the very idea was preposterous.

I made a mental note to steer clear of Chez Cuisine. Rats or not, I didn't feel like I really needed to take in any atmosphere Davies created. Still, a good neighbor is often a quiet neighbor, so I listened attentively and then asked his suggestion for the cookbooks we should carry. "It's about time someone asked my expertise on things around this town," he said as he snatched the notebook and pen from my hand and headed toward the cooking section.

I caught Rocky's eye in the café, and she doubled over laughing. Guess Davies had a reputation.

Traffic into the shop kept the bell over the door dinging steadily, and I barely had time to help customers find books they might like – my favorite part of the job – before I had to ring up another sale. I knew it wouldn't last forever this way, but I was pretty excited still. Last night's quick tally showed we made a really good net profit for our first day, and today looked like it might be even better. At this rate, I might even be able to hire a clerk to help so that I didn't have to be at the shop every minute it was open . . . although I kind of wanted to be, at least for now.

At one point in the afternoon, I came to the surprising discovery that many of the books in both of my window displays had been purchased, so I flagged down Mart as she hustled about straightening shelves and answering questions and asked her to cover the register for me so I could restock. One or two books missing from a window display made the shop look good; only one or two left made it look derelict.

I headed to the storeroom, bracing myself to enter. I'd been avoiding the space. But my extra copies of Catherine Clinton's book were in there, and I thought I had a few more gardening titles that I'd been saving for later in the spring.

I stepped inside and let out the breath I'd been holding. The room looked normal, very normal in fact. No police tape. No chalk outline on the floor. Nothing at all to indicate that a person had died there. The business owner in me was glad of that, but the person who loved people, she was sad. I sat down gently on a box of cups for the café and took a moment. I knew Stevensmith wasn't here – she didn't seem the type to haunt a simple bookstore. If her spirit was lingering, it had grander aspirations – but I still felt like saying something was in order. "Ms. Stevensmith, I know you found my little shop lacking, but I still appreciate that you came and wrote about us. Thank you."

I heard a rustle to my left and jumped up to see who was there. A tiny, white woman in a polka dot raincoat was in the doorway. "Can I help you?"

"Oh, I'm sorry, dear. I didn't mean to startle you. I was looking for the bathroom, but I see I've made a wrong turn."

I hustled over to her. "Of course. Let me show you the way." I gestured behind her, but she didn't move.

"Lucia actually liked your shop, you know? I know she didn't show that well, but she was thrilled that you were opening. 'About time we had a bookstore in St. Marin's,' she said."

I stepped back so I could look the woman in the face. "You knew Ms. Stevensmith?"

"Well, of course I did, dear. I'm her mother."

I took a step backward in surprise. "Oh my goodness. I'm so

sorry." Fatigue and embarrassment made me fumble my words. "I didn't know – I'm so sorry for your loss."

The woman put a tiny hand on my arm. "It's fine, dear. You're new. How would you know? I'm Divina Stevensmith. It's nice to meet you."

I laid my hand over hers and found her skin was ice cold. "You're freezing. Can I get you a cup of something hot?"

She smiled. "Maybe after I go to the bathroom?"

"Oh yes, of course. Right this way." I closed the storeroom door behind me and walked her to the other side of the shop and pointed at the door. "Right there. I'll wait for you here, if that's okay, and then maybe we can have coffee and you can tell me a bit more about Ms., I mean Lucia."

She nodded and headed to the door in small, graceful steps. I turned back to the store to wait, but then got pulled away by a customer looking for a book that would encourage her fourteen-year-old son to read. By the time I got back, the bathroom door was ajar and Ms. Stevensmith was nowhere to be seen.

After a quick glance around the shop to see if I could spot her brightly colored rain coat, I headed back to the storeroom to grab the books for the window displays. The door wasn't shut tight, and I was pretty sure I'd closed it all the way. That felt off, but then, maybe Rocky had come in for supplies for the café or something. I didn't have time to worry over nothing, so I grabbed my books, and headed back out with a stack of titles up to my chin.

Chapter Four

By close on Sunday, my whole body ached, and I was more tired than I thought I'd ever been, but I was giddy, too. The weekend's sales had given my bank accounts a boost, but more importantly, I was feeling confident that I could do this thing, that I might not have to mooch off of Mart forever.

I stayed behind at the store after everyone left just to straighten up and to enjoy the quiet for a bit. I reshelved all the books that had been left around over the weekend. I checked the picture books in the kids' section to be sure no dust jackets were torn. I gave Mayhem a good rub on her bed by the register. I fussed with the chairs in the perfectly tidy café just so I could put a hand to everything in the shop.

Then, I dropped into the wingback chair next to the poetry section and cried. Being super tired always made me a little weepy, but I was also immensely grateful for all the ways my friends and the people of St. Marin's had rallied around my little store. Gratitude made me weepy, too.

I was finishing up my private crying jag when I heard a knock at the window and realized, with a shudder, that everyone on the street could see me since I had left all the lights on. Tomorrow would be fun. "Why were you crying, Harvey?" "Everything okay, Harvey?" Sigh.

Mayhem came to my side as I got up and went to the front of the shop. I shielded my eyes so I could see past the reflection of the Edison bulbs, and I felt my mortification grow. There stood Daniel and Taco. Mayhem must have smelled her friend because her tail started wagging a mile a minute. I, however, wanted to disappear into the bookshelves never to return.

Daniel gestured to the door and then to himself, and I nodded. Might as well let him know I'm okay. Maybe he could spread the word.

I unlocked the door, and Taco trotted on in and gave Mayhem a sniff before they headed to the café to be sure Rocky and I had tended to all the crumbs. Daniel locked the door behind him with my keys that were hanging there and then looked at me. "Big weekend. Just decompressing, I imagine."

I smiled. That's precisely what it had been – a release – and I was heartened that he knew that. "Exactly. Most of my strong emotions – good and hard – come out as tears. I've just always been that way."

"I get it. I kind of think you might be healthier than a lot of us since you just let it all out."

"Well, thanks for that." I tried to suppress a ridiculous grin. "You okay?"

"Oh yeah, just out walking the canine slug. He usually has a pass up and back on Main before he totally refuses to walk further and I carry him the rest of the way home."

"Wow. He's not a lightweight pup. Maybe you should trade him in for a Pomeranian if you're going to have to carry him."

Daniel laughed. "Nah, no trade-ins. He's stuck with me. I have contemplated a wagon though." He shifted the leash from one hand to the other. "When I saw the lights on here, I thought maybe you and Mayhem would like to walk with us."

I glanced over at our dogs, who had now taken up resting positions back to back by the front window. "Looks like they're game.

Just let me get my coat. But I should be clear – I'm not carrying anyone. Everyone gets home on their own power."

"Understood. You hear that, Taco? The lady is not hefting your big butt." Taco wagged his tail.

Outside, the air was brisk, and I worried for the daffodils that had begun showing their sunny faces in the warm sun of the weekend. Mayhem's leash rested lightly around my right wrist as I pulled on my mittens. "Ready to go when you are. Were you on your way up Main Street or back?"

"Back. I was hoping you and Mayhem would motivate Taco to go a bit further, but I didn't want to take my chances that his enthusiasm would wear off too soon and you'd have to see me try to lift him."

I laughed. "He doesn't look light," I said as I eyed the sizable belly on the low-slung pooch.

"He isn't."

We walked along in comfortable silence for a bit, and I enjoyed the chance to look into the shop windows and admire the window displays. Even Heron's farm stand was decked out for spring with beautiful 3-D flowers made from folded paper taped to the windows and attached to wooden dowels in vases in the sills. "Ms. Heron seems nice," I said almost to myself.

"She is, although I'm not sure most folks would call her nice."

I gave him a look.

"Oh, I don't mean that she's not kind. Just that she's a force. You know she runs her farm and this farm stand by herself? Sometimes for harvest, she hires local teenagers, but mostly, she does it all – the planting, the weeding, the marketing. I don't think she sleeps."

She had looked tired when she'd stopped by the shop today to check on our order of daffodils for the café tables. "That must be exhausting. Just the shop tires me out, and I don't have to grow the books myself."

We reached the end of Main Street, and I felt a little sad that our walk hadn't lasted longer. But I was tired and wanted to get home before the fatigue turned my legs and my brain to mush. "This is my turn," I said, pointing east.

"Ah, you're on the water side."

"I am. That was one of the requirements for wherever I lived – a water view. I got spoiled in San Francisco with water on three sides of the city and the Pacific Ocean and Golden Gate within walking distance of my apartment. Plus, I love this water. I grew up on the Bay. It'll always be home."

"I didn't know you were from around here."

"Well not here exactly. Just up the road in Cecil County, Chesapeake City."

"I love that town. Did they build the canal through it, or did the town just grow up around the canal?"

"The canal brought the town, definitely." I thought about the charming town that I'd hated in high school. No teenager likes for everyone to know everything about you.

I looked up into his face. He was smiling, and his face was so kind. "Thanks for this, Daniel. It was really nice."

"Agreed. Maybe another evening we can do it again . . . or even take a walk by the water."

I grinned. "I'd like that. Have a good night." I gave Mayhem a tug and headed down the street to our house, eager to tell Mart, well, everything. Suddenly, I didn't feel quite as tired.

Monday morning came early, but I woke with gusto. A new shipment of books was coming in, and I couldn't wait to open the boxes, smell the ink and paper, and get shelving. There's just something so satisfying about putting things away, and when those things are bound collections of stories and information, it's even more fun, at least to me.

Rocky came in not long after I arrived at the store, this time with a tray full of cookies. "Your mom was baking again?"

"Oh, I made these. I was so keyed up from the weekend that I couldn't sleep. So I baked. Spring-themed sugar cookies."

I walked over to take a look and saw an assortment of flowers and rabbits. "These are beautiful. You decorated these by hand?"

A blush spread over Rocky's cheeks. "I did. I'm just learning, but I think they came out okay."

"Okay? These are amazing! And I bet they taste as good as they look."

She turned toward the counter with a smile. "Let me get the coffee brewed, and we'll find out."

"I like how you think."

Today was going to be the first day Rocky and I were on our own. Mart had to spend some time at the winery and then she was off to the mainland to consult with a winery up in Westminster. Over breakfast, she'd offered to stay home. "Or I can drive back tonight. I'll do that. It'll be fine. I'll just caffeinate—"

"Mart, you will do no such thing. We will be fine. I will be fine. I have my trusty sidekick here," I gave Mayhem a nudge with my foot, "And I have friends in town if I need them."

"Friends like Daniel."

I rolled my eyes. "What are we, twelve?"

"When it comes to boys, yes, we are twelve." She grabbed her briefcase and headed toward the door. "You'll call if you need me?"

"I won't need you, but yes, and you'll text when you get to your hotel?"

"Sure, Mom." She gave me a kiss on the cheek and headed out the door.

Now, I was missing her presence in the shop. Having her there made me sure of myself, confident that she'd have my back. But I took a deep breath, glanced over at Rocky, and steadied my shoulders. We had this.

We opened at ten a.m., and within moments, a few folks had come in to grab coffee from the café. No real book shopping happened on Monday mornings, I knew. Most of us had too much ahead of us in the week to think about reading, but I enjoyed the chance to catch up on the industry news, check out upcoming releases, and brainstorm a few ideas for author events.

I had a quirky notion for a "Welcome to Spring" celebration for late March, and I wanted to see if I might be able to get David Healey, a local author, down for a reading from his Delmarva Renovators mystery series. His books were set in my hometown, and I thought I could probably get a good crowd from there and here in for the event, especially if the restaurants in town might do a special something for folks coming to the reading. I got to giggling as I thought about how Max Davies might try to redeem his chewy snails.

I was so focused on how we could do a murder mystery party after dinner that I was surprised when someone cleared their throat just on the other side of the counter.

I looked up to see Sheriff Mason grinning at me. "You are enjoying yourself, huh?"

I blushed. "I am. Planning some events for the store. It's really fun. Do you like mysteries?"

"Live them every day, so I'd say so."

"Ah yes." I closed my laptop and came out from behind the counter. "What can I do for you?"

"I just wanted to update you on the investigation."

"Oh, right. Okay. Do you want to sit in the café?" I scanned the shop. Just one woman browsing in the poetry section, so I was pretty sure I had a few minutes. Poetry readers are devoted, but the books weren't our hottest ticket.

We took a seat by the garage door that I'd had converted to mostly glass, and Rocky brought us two cappuccinos – she knew the sheriff's preference – with little flowers in the foam. "Very cute," Mason said with a chuckle.

"Thanks. I figured you needed something adorable in your day."

"Always," he said as he took a long swig from the mug. "Delicious. This from that roaster down in Easton? – because it's amazing."

"Yep." I had been thrilled to see that a local company was roasting coffee right on the Eastern Shore and had arranged to get all our beans from them. I liked to keep things as local as I could.

I watched Rocky walk back to the counter to wait on her next customer before I leaned over and asked, "Okay, so what's the story?"

"Not much story, I'm afraid. You already knew Stevensmith had been hit and had probably come in here to hide. That's still our best theory. We do know that she was clobbered with something that left a curved mark in her skull, but we still don't know what that something was."

I leaned back in my chair and sipped my drink. "Man, that's not much to go on."

"No. No, it's not," the sheriff scooted in, "but this helps." He slid a little plastic bag toward me.

I picked it up and pulled it close to my face. "A piece of bright orange paper? Okay, fill me in."

"I brought it by because I thought it might be a piece from a book cover, something that might give us a bit more of the story about Stevensmith's steps that night."

I scrutinized the triangular sliver again. "I can't say as I recognize that color or that paper texture from any of our books or even from the little bit of stationery we stock." I pointed to a spinning rack near the register. "I don't think this came from here."

He smiled.

"I thought you'd be disappointed," I said.

"Oh no. If it's not from here, then it's from somewhere else, and that somewhere else might just be the murder scene."

He scraped his chair back from the table and stood. "Thanks, Harvey. I'll keep you updated as I'm able. But of course, you know I can't really talk about too many details."

"Of course. And as I find info, I'll pass it on, too."

"As you find info? Harvey, you know Williams and I can handle this, right?"

We began walking toward the front door. "Of course, I do. I'm just nosy I guess."

"Well, nosy can be dangerous. Best to let us do the nosing around, okay?"

I shivered, remembering all too well how true his statement was. "I'll do my best."

He shook his head. "You're a stubborn one."

"You better believe it. Wouldn't be here," I did a little spin in the shop, "if that wasn't the case?"

I could hear the sheriff laughing as he walked to his SUV.

I spent the rest of the morning ordering books to replace those we had sold over the weekend, and I even bulked up our inventory a bit with the profit we'd made. But in the back of my mind, I was trying to figure out just why that particular shade of orange had seemed so familiar.

———

That afternoon, I was just reorganizing the religion section – those spiritual folks could de-alphabetize shelves like nobody's business – when I heard the bell chime. I pried myself up off the floor from among the stacks of books and stepped out, right into a woman about my age with a long, ponytail of silver hair. "Oh, I'm so sorry. Goodness, you're quick. I just heard you come in."

"I'm so sorry. I want to shop, but can I—"

"Yep, just over there. Door on the left." I had been that person chagrined but in need when it came to a bathroom. When I opened the shop, I vowed to never refuse its use to anyone. It was just so mortifying to have to bounce around while you waited in line to get a key.

I went back to reshelving until I felt a hand on my back and stood to see the woman standing beside me. "Thank you so much. You have no idea."

"Oh, I expect I have some idea. Been there, done that. Happy to help."

"Well, thank you." She extended a hand and then smiled. "I did wash."

I took her hand. "I'm Harvey. This is my shop."

"I'm so glad to meet you, Harvey, and so glad you're here. Ever since I moved to St. Marin's a few years back, I've thought we needed a bookstore. I'm Cate."

I detected a little Deep South accent in this slightly plump and very stylish Asian woman. "So you're not from here then?"

"Oh no. I moved up from Atlanta about eight years ago. My husband directs the maritime museum, and I paint."

"Oh, did I need you last week?" I gestured toward the white-washed brick and then gave Cate a sideways wink. "Just kidding. What do you paint?"

She laughed. "You'd be surprised how many calls I get to give estimates on painting barns." She looked at me intently. "Or maybe you wouldn't. I expect not much gets past you." She smiled. "I paint landscapes mostly, a lot of scenes of the water here, obviously. But my passion is portraits."

"That's interesting. Do you get commissions for portraits often?"

"Nope. But that's okay with me. I'm not much for sitting in a room painting someone else sitting in a room. My preference is to do portraits of people as they work. The watermen around here – those old-timers who have been on a boat every day of every decade in their life – their faces have so much story in there."

I knew then and there that Cate and I would be good friends. Anyone who can see the story in a person's face was someone I wanted to know.

"Maybe sometime you'd let me paint you?" she asked with a steady gaze at my face.

I turned away and grabbed a stack of Barbara Brown Taylor books. "Why me? My face has been in a cubicle for most of the last twenty years. Not much story there."

"Oh, I know that's not true. I can see it at the edges of your eyes."

"Ah, the crow's feet tell the tale."

"Something like that," Cate said. "Now, where's your art section?"

She and I spent the rest of the afternoon looking at art books with her guiding me to some new ones I should add to give the section a good foundation and pointing out others that I might want to return since they didn't have the best quality images or because she knew that the artists hadn't been fairly compensated for their work in the pages. I was usually loathe to return books, even though I got reimbursed for what I'd spent on them, but if the artists had been cheated, that was a no brainer.

By the time we'd reviewed the whole section and I'd rung up the couple dozen customers who had come through – almost everyone who came in bought something, a true kindness from my neighbors – it was getting dark and was almost time to close up shop. "Oh my word, I've been here all day, and I really just stopped in to say hello, pick up the latest issue of *Where Women Create*, and of course, pee. I'm so sorry for taking all your time." Cate pulled out the hair tie and smoothed her hair back into its sleek ponytail.

"Oh gracious, please. I had a great time, and you really helped me with that art section. Thank you."

"Not sure how much help I was," she said picking up the magazine she'd come for, one of my favorites, too, "but it's almost dinner time. If you don't have plans, come on home with me, meet Lucas, and have dinner. Mondays are always pasta nights, so we can fortify for the week ahead."

Mart had texted to say she was safe and sound in Westminster, and I had been planning on a bowl of cereal for dinner. This sounded far better. "Sure. Thanks. I'll just close up here, drop Mayhem off at home," as if on cue, the pooch stretched and squeaked with pleasure, "then I'll be there."

"Yay. I'll help you close up, and please bring Mayhem. Our little Sasquatch loves other dogs."

I let out a burst of a laugh. "You have a dog named Sasquatch."

"Sure do. He's a miniature Schnauzer. All fur and personality."

It didn't take us long to help Rocky wipe down the café tables, and I turned out the lights as the three of us headed toward the door. "Rocky, want to join us?" Cate asked as we stepped out onto the sidewalk.

"Oh, thank you, but I need to get home and do homework. Plus, Mama made her curry soup, and I cannot miss that goodness."

"No ma'am, you cannot," Cate said.

Most everything in the town of St. Marin's was within walking distance, so when we turned up a side street away from the water – *toward Daniel's side of town*, I found myself thinking – I was delighted. I loved this street with its rambling Victorians towering above cute Craftsman cottages. Mart and I had thought about buying something small on this very lane, but the lure of the water had taken me a few blocks away, over by where the museum was. We strolled to the far end of the street, and Cate led us up the sidewalk to the most wonderfully out-of-place home on the block. It was a lean, angular modern building clad in long, thin planks of what looked like bamboo. Windows were scattered about the front in a pattern that I liked, but couldn't describe. The trim on all the windows was a gunmetal gray, and the front yard was covered in wood chips with a shrub here and there.

"In the summer, this yard becomes a meadow of wildflowers. It's a nice contrast to the hard lines of the modern house design. Sort of like Lucas and me. He spends so much time with old things at work that he really wanted to come home to something that only had our story attached, so we built this home when we moved here. The wildflowers are my way of softening our space, blending us in a bit."

"I love it," I said and meant it. "Did the neighbors object?" I could see how some of St. Marin's more, um, traditional community members might have found the sleek design – and maybe the wild-flowers too – in poor taste since they didn't match the historical design of most of the town.

"There was some grumbling of course. Always is in a small town. But people like Lucas so much, they pretty much stayed quiet." Cate's voice was matter-of-fact – even. She clearly didn't let much get to her.

As we went in through the full-glass double doors, I gasped. "Oh my goodness. It's so beautiful." The doors opened into a long, wide hallway with a view to the dining room and kitchen and beyond that a full wall of windows that looked out over the brackish canal that ran behind the house. In the half-light, I could see two egrets and a great blue heron standing sentry in the reeds. "That window." I walked right to it and stared.

I heard a deep chuckle to my left and turned with embarrassment. There, apron over his khakis and polo, was a man I took to be Lucas. He was tall – well over six feet – and thin, reed-like is how I could describe him. "The view gets everyone the first time."

He put down the pasta spoon he had been holding, wiped his hands on the apron, and came to greet me. "I'm Lucas. Nice to meet you."

"I brought home my new friend. I expect you made enough pasta," Cate said as she flung her wool cape over the back of a club chair in the living room just in front of the kitchen.

"I'm Harvey," I said with a smile. "And that's Mayhem." My pup was doing the usual sniff and greet with the most adorable dog I'd ever seen. "This must be Sasquatch. I love his eyebrows."

"Nice to meet you, Harvey. Someday I need to know the story of that name. And yes, that's our resident pillow stealer. Guard yours if you ever stay over. You've been warned," he said as he headed back to his work. "Pasta puttanesca okay? I felt like capers today, and Merv down at the fish market had some amazing anchovies."

I tried not to wince. I wasn't the biggest fan of seafood, which made me ridiculous in this town where dinner was literally out the window. Something in my face must have given me away because Cate asked, "Not a big fan of anchovies?"

"Not really. I don't like much fish, actually."

Lucas gasped with mock horror. "That's it. You'll have to leave," he said with a smile. "Just kidding. Lucky for you, I cook the anchovies separately so I can mince them over the top, so I'll just leave them off your plate."

I sighed with relief. "Thanks. If you have a tiny bit I can try, I'm always game. Just anchovies . . . "

"They're the stuff of pizza nightmares, I know." Lucas turned the big saucepan full of pasta and veggies with tongs. "Trust me, these are not *those* anchovies."

"Wine?" Cate said holding up a glass.

"Yes, please."

She poured me a glass of a gorgeous pinot noir, and I savored my first sip. Then, Lucas plated our food and we sat down at their long, blonde table. The conversation wandered from Lucas's work at the museum to my shop to Cate's plan for a series of portraits of the oldest residents in St. Marin's.

By the time I was done with my second glass of wine, had decided anchovies weren't totally terrible, and gobbled down a vanilla cupcake that Lucas had picked up from the bakery in town, I was completely relaxed and felt right at home. I couldn't wait to introduce Mart to Cate and Lucas.

I looked at my phone and saw it was after ten. "Oh my. I better get home and feed this girl." I looked down at Mayhem, who was asleep on her side at my feet, and gave her a nudge.

"Actually, I think she and Sas shared dinner. Hope you don't mind."

"Are you kidding? Anyone who will feed me and my dog is a friend for life."

Cate stood with me and grabbed my peacoat off the chair. "Thank you for coming. I'm so glad you're part of our town, Harvey." Her face grew more serious. "I know the shop got off to a rough start."

I had almost forgotten about the murder, which I felt kind of bad about. "Did you know Ms. Stevensmith?"

"I did," Lucas said as they walked me to the door. "She was an acquired taste, let's say."

"That's how most everybody describes her. My experience was similar."

"Still, it's a tragedy," Cate said quietly.

"It is. The sheriff says they're making progress on the investigation." I didn't know how much I could share of what the sheriff had told me, so I kept it simple.

"Good. I don't like the idea of having a murderer in our little town." Cate shuddered.

"And on that note, let me run you home, Harvey. It's late, and I would feel better if you weren't walking alone." Lucas was already grabbing his coat.

I smiled gratefully. "What? You don't think this girl can protect me?" I gave the sleepy dog a nudge with my ankle.

"Oh, I'm sure she would. But what if she hurts someone else? Best to just keep all our citizens, even the canine ones, safe."

As Lucas and I drove the few blocks to my house, he caught me up on all the quirky people in town. There was the guy who pretended to be homeless when the tourists were around and made a good enough living to afford his Bentley in the off-season. And the woman who wore only purple ever. "Rumor has it that *everything* she wears is purple."

I guffawed. "Hey, maybe you can tell me about someone I met briefly the other day. Black kid, late teens or early twenties, a really impressive flat top?"

"Oh, you met Marcus." Lucas's voice had lost all the humor. "Marcus Dawson. He went to Salisbury U for a few years. Rumor has it that he was uber-smart, too smart for his own good, maybe. For whatever reason, he flunked out and moved to St. Marin's. He does odd jobs for folks – hard worker for sure – but kind of angry."

"Hmmm. He was pleasant enough for me, but he did use up at least two whole rolls of paper towels in the bathroom at the shop."

"Hmph. Maybe he doesn't have great aim?"

I laughed hard as Lucas pulled up to my house. I loved this town.

Chapter Five

The next morning, Mayhem and I took a little more circuitous route to the shop. That little piece of paper that Sheriff Mason had mentioned had come to mind as I scrambled an egg that morning – it might have been the turmeric that I threw in for flavor that triggered some hint of a memory, something to do with Main Street. So the hound and I headed out early to see if we could find the source of that nibble.

We walked past the park on the waterfront and took a left through our neighborhood of ranchers and cottages that were the homes to some of St. Marin's year-round residents. We hung a right on Main Street and went past the sail shop, the garden center, and the stately historic houses that had probably been home to ship builders back in the nineteenth century. As we passed the bookstore, I could see Rocky inside dancing, and I smiled.

We strolled on up the block past the post office and the creperie, where the smell of sizzling butter almost drew me in. A couple was looking at the real estate listings at the broker's office on the corner, and I found myself hoping they could afford the high price of our gorgeous town's real estate because we could use a few more young families in the area. I peeked in Max Davies's windows at the quaint tables for two and found myself actually wanting to eat there, despite the owner's bristly personality.

Ahead, I could see Eleanor Heron opening the front shutters on her farm stand, and that's when I remembered – the paper flowers in her windows. I tried to keep my pace steady as Mayhem and I walked over to Eleanor, whose arms were full of something that looked like plump bowling pins.

"Hey Harvey. Hey, Mayhem." She put her load down in the bins just inside the door and bent down to give the dog a scratch. "Just putting out the last of my winter squash. I ration these all winter so I have produce throughout the cold months. Need to keep that foot traffic going," she said with a laugh. "I expect you'll know more about that soon enough."

"I expect I will," I said with a smile as I stepped over to the leaded glass windows. "Tell me about these flowers, Eleanor. They're gorgeous."

"Aren't they, though? They sell them over there at the art co-op," she said as she came and stood next to me. "I bought these years ago and just keep them in a tote for the first hint of spring. But I saw they had some there again this year when I stopped by the other day . . . you know, if you want some for your shop."

I gave her a big grin. "I might just do that for when I put up my spring picture book display." I took a step toward the door. "I know you're not technically open yet, but would you mind if I took a closer look, see what I might be getting for my money."

"Sure thing." Eleanor held the door open for me. "I'll just be in the back. Have a few cases of honey and locally made mustard to put out. Those folks here for the festival cleaned me out."

I tried to recall the exact color of orange that had been in that corner of paper the sheriff had showed me as I gazed at the intricately-folded blooms. Each one was a little different, and they were exquisite. I could see why the art co-op sold them – each was a little masterpiece in and of itself.

I couldn't tell, though, if the oranges in some of the paper were the same as the one the sheriff had, though. Hmph. I had hoped this would be a good solid lead. Still, it was something.

"Thanks so much, Eleanor," I shouted as Mayhem and I headed for the door. "They really are beautiful."

"Call me Elle," she said from the back. "All my friends do. I'll be up to your shop later. I have a couple books I'd like to order."

"See you soon then."

We scooted over Main Street toward the art co-op, but a sign on the door said they didn't open until noon, and I needed to get my shop open anyway; it was almost ten. I made a mental note to check back later.

The day in the shop went by lickety-split between customers and the usual book deliveries for Tuesday. Tuesday is the day most of the new books come out, so I made a lot of displays of titles that I'd convinced publishers would sell here, even in a new store, including a new mystery novel from Baltimore's Laura Lippman, who was adored by most Marylanders.

When I finally took a break about mid-afternoon to check my email, I was delighted to see a note from my friends Stephen and Walter back in San Francisco. They were wondering if they could come out that weekend for a visit. It didn't even take me a second to send back a yes with approximately thirty exclamation points and the address. Oh, it would be so good to have them here. They'd wanted to come for the grand opening, but Stephen had a big fundraising event with our old organization the same day and couldn't miss it. Anyway, it was kind of nice to have them come when there was a little less excitement. I could enjoy my time with them more this way.

I also had a note from my parents. They, too, had missed the grand opening, but unlike my friends, they hadn't offered to come visit. They'd been down from Chesapeake City once, not long after Mart and I had moved in. They'd rented a room at the fancy B&B in town, even though we'd offered to let them stay in our guest room, and when they'd seen the shop location – which did still look remarkably like a gas station at that point – they'd said, "Oh, I hope you didn't pay too much."

This note was typical Burt and Sharon Beckett. I knew they wrote to feel like they were being good parents, checking in on their daughter who now lived less than an hour away. But they didn't really open up any space for me to tell them how I actually was. It was more a "thinking of you" because we know we're supposed to than a "How are you really?" kind of a note. I wrote back the required and equally distant response to thank them, tell them I was fine, and note that I'd met Catherine Clinton. A little dig at my history-buff father and a note about my own success, too. I hit send with a little zing down my arm.

It would have been easy to get bitter about my parents – justified, too – but I had decided a long time ago that they were who they were, and that meant they just weren't going to "get" me. Somehow, they had raised a daughter who didn't value the things they did – notoriety and financial stability – and that disappointed them. But I liked who I was, and now that I was on my own again after a marriage that was stable but broken in a really fundamental way, I finally was able to live the life I wanted to live. In fact, I'd signed my divorce papers just last week, so even the pesky legal part was over. My life was my own, and, even if it disappointed my parents, I was going to live it my way.

The last email in my inbox was from Max Davies. I'd sent him a note the day before asking if he'd think about creating a special dinner for my Welcome to Spring dinner, and to my surprise and pleasure, he thought the idea was wonderful. "I'll come up with a *Prix Fixe* menu and keep the price reasonable by asking my vendors to consider a break for the cause. I love, especially, that you want to donate to the humane society. I'd be honored to be a part, and so would Gertrude. Thank you for inviting us." He signed off with a picture of a very fluffy, very confident cat, who I could only presume was Gertrude.

I couldn't help but smile. Maybe Max wasn't so prickly after all.

At the end of the day, Rocky and I closed up shop, and as we walked out, Rocky jerked me out of the way as a blur whizzed by.

"Watch where you're going," she shouted, the blur stopped and turned back. It was Marcus Dawson.

"Sorry. Didn't see you," he said with a quick wave before dropping his board to the ground again.

Something about what Lucas had told me about him made me want to reach out to the kid, so before he could skate off, I said, "Hey Marcus. I could use some help around the shop this week. Come by if you'd like the work."

He paused then and turned to face me.

"No pressure. Just if you want it." I was suddenly nervous that I'd overstepped, offended him in some way.

He studied me a second more and then said, "See you tomorrow." Then, he was off.

Rocky gave me a small smile. "Your heart is so big, Harvey. Just be wise."

I hugged her and started walking toward home. I kept looking around, hopeful. Maybe Daniel was going to come by to walk me home again. But as I walked, I felt my disappointment growing. Then I chided myself for being foolish – both for expecting him to show and for being so hopeful he would. *He just said he might come by, Harvey. No promises.*

By the time I got home, I felt a bit better. The walk through a brisk evening had helped, as did the beauty of the town with its quaint gardens and houses with golden light coming through their front windows. Sometimes, I felt like I'd moved to the set for a 1950s sitcom . . . or maybe a Perry Mason episode, given the murder that had me preoccupied. I kept thinking about the shape of the blow to Stevensmith's head and trying to figure out what someone could wield with enough force to leave a mark. I felt like it would have been suspicious if the murderer had been carrying a pipe around town, and it was just too much like a game of *Clue* to imagine a candlestick. What would leave that mark? And what about that piece of orange paper? I needed more information.

———

The next morning, Mart came with me to the shop to help open. Rocky had classes on Wednesday mornings, so Mart had arranged her work schedule so that she could cover the café until Rocky got back around one. Talk about a good friend.

Marcus showed up just after we opened for the day, and I was impressed. I'd randomly shouted an offer for work at him on the street, and he'd still followed through. I liked a person of their word. I set him to work cleaning up the weeds behind the shop. I felt bad because I didn't have a weed eater or anything, but when I mentioned that I could try to borrow one, he'd said, "Nah. Sometimes, it's better to work with my hands anyway."

I liked this kid . . . but I kept thinking about how Lucas had said he was kind of angry. I hadn't seen any signs of that, but I was keeping my eye out.

Given the sparse number of shoppers first thing in the day, I took the opportunity to slip over to the art co-op while Mart staffed the book register and café. I promised I wouldn't be gone longer than a half-hour. Mayhem and I buzzed up the street, giving polite nods instead of the usual stops to chat, and when we turned into the co-op, we were greeted by a cheerful yip from Sasquatch. I looked up to see Cate behind the desk, a phone to her ear. She smiled and held up one finger. I nodded and tied Mayhem up beside Sasquatch near the front door.

While Cate finished her call, I browsed the art in the various studio windows inside. It wasn't a big building – a former warehouse of some sort, I thought – but I counted at least ten studios. One older, white gentleman was throwing something that looked to be a very thin, very beautiful vase on a potter's wheel, and a young Latinx person stood at a giant canvas adding bright dashes of blue and turquoise. A tiny white woman bent over a table covered in black velvet, a jeweler's loupe to her eye, and a tall, lean black woman was weaving at the biggest loom I'd ever seen. She saw me watching and waved me over. I smiled and headed her way just as Cate caught up to me.

"Henrietta Johnson is one of the finest weavers on the East Coast."

"You flatter, Cate, you flatter. Keep it up." She put down the slim piece of wood she'd been holding and reached over to shake my hand. "I am Henrietta, but everyone calls me Henri."

"Henri, I'm Harvey." I put out my hand with a grin.

"Another woman with a man's name. Your given one?"

"Nope. Anastasia Lovejoy."

"My word. Now that's a name. I'd go with Harvey, too." I liked Henri already.

I leaned a bit closer to Henri's weaving. "May I?" I asked as I put my hand over the cloth.

"Please do. And thanks for asking. So many people just assume they can touch things. It's cashmere from goats just up the street. The farmer cleans it for me, and then she spins it up so I can dye it and then weave it."

"It's so soft. I want to put my face on it."

Henri laughed. "Me, too. That's why I make a lot of pillows. But trust me, you don't want to sleep on this stuff. It'll clog up your sinuses like nobody's business."

"Got it." I gave the weaving one last caress and then smiled. "Nice to meet you, Henri."

"You, too. I'll be down by your shop later. Been meaning to stop in. Now I've got a reason. It's my turn to lay hands on your work."

"Perfect," I said.

Cate tucked her arm in mine as we headed back to the front desk. "To what do we owe this pleasure?"

"Well, I was hoping you might have some of those paper flowers that Eleanor has up in her shop."

"Oh yeah, this way. You want some for your shop?"

"Well, um, no." I told her about Sheriff Mason and the slip of paper.

She stopped in the hallway outside of a small studio tucked at the back of the co-op building. "So you think the person who made the flowers murdered Stevensmith? Wow, that would be something considering."

"Considering what?"

"Considering that Divina Stevensmith is the one who makes

them." She pointed to the name tag on the door of the studio. "D. Stevensmith."

"No way. That's too easy, isn't it? I mean, really."

Cate shrugged. "How should I know? I've never tried to solve a murder before." I let out a long sigh.

"I don't know anything. Don't even know that the paper is from her flowers. It just struck me as a possibility."

"Well, let's see what we can find out, shall we?" She knocked once and then opened the door of Divina Stevensmith's studio.

I gasped as we walked in. The room was a bright burst of color, like confetti was suspended in time and space around us. It was beautiful.

"Divina, I think you met Harvey, the owner of our very own bookstore. She came to ask about your flowers."

Mrs. Stevensmith dropped off a high stool behind the high table where she'd been working and came across the floor to meet me. She grinned and grabbed my left hand, squeezing it firmly. "It's good to see you again, dear."

"This," I spun around slowly, "this is amazing. You did this?" I kept staring at the mobiles of paper that hung from every level of the ceiling and made a forest of color around me.

"I did. This is my mind writ large. All color moving freely in space. I call it my Miasma of Beauty."

"Oh, I like that," I said and meant it.

I studied a few more of the flowers hanging in the air around us and then moved past them to pick up some of the folded blooms attached to green paper stems like the ones I'd seen at Eleanor's farm stand. "I love these, Mrs. Stevensmith. Do you ever do them in orange?"

"Orange. No, never. I hate that color. Vulgar." The tiny woman's voice rang off the walls.

The ferocious shift in the woman's tone caught me off-guard, and I shot Cate a quick glance. She gave her shoulders a little shrug.

"Oh, okay. I was going to ask for a few of them . . . and also see if you might have a source for orange paper for something I'm planning at the shop this summer."

The thin woman turned her back to me. "I do not. I hate that color and would never have a thing to do with it. Never." The venom in her words made them sharp, and I kept hoping she'd turn around so I could see if she was joking. But she didn't. Instead, she began massacring pieces of thick paper with shiny, silver scissors. She *really* hated the color orange.

Then, her furious paper-cutting stopped, and she turned halfway back towards us. "But you know, Max Davies might have an idea. He used to have those horrendous orange menus. You remember them, don't you dear?" She turned to face Cate then, and I caught what I thought was a glimmer of a smile. "They were the color and texture of orange peel. Disgusting."

I turned to Cate. "Oh yeah, he did have orange menus, I guess, a while back." She gave me another shrug.

"Alright. Well, I'll ask him then. Thanks."

Mrs. Stevensmith turned back to the rear of her studio silently, and we took that as our not-so-subtle cue to step out.

As we headed back to the desk, Cate gave me a wink and said, "Divina, always a character."

I laughed . . . but I wasn't sure I found it charming.

I untied Mayhem as I left the co-op and was just heading back toward the shop when a sound like a foghorn caught in a tunnel lit up the street and I turned to see Taco baying for all his worth across the street. Daniel was hurrying out of the hardware store with a small, white bag in hand, and I could hear him saying, "Taco, stop that. Taco. Taco!"

As Taco saw his person, the energy from his mouth traveled right down to his tail, and I saw two passersby wince when it smacked them in the legs. I couldn't help but smile . . . until Mayhem started barking at her friend and Taco got going again. Suddenly, it was a two-dog cacophony on the street, and everyone looked back and forth from one dog to the other.

I started walking Mayhem down the street, but she locked her legs straight and dug in. It was like trying to walk a stool, so I stopped and looked back at Taco. Daniel was staring back at us, and I felt the color rush to my face. Then, a smile broke across his lips, and I smiled back, and soon we were both doubled over laughing while our dogs continued to bray. Eventually, he got enough control to hold up one finger to signal me and then get Taco to the crosswalk at the corner.

By the time the pair reached me, I had almost regained my composure, well, at least about the spectacle. I could feel my heart racing, but hopefully, Daniel couldn't tell. "Where you headed?" he asked as Mayhem and Taco did the usual meet-and-greet.

"Back to the shop. Treat you to a cup of coffee." I grinned and hoped my invitation sounded casual.

"Sounds good. We have a few minutes before Mrs. Fenster brings in her ancient Mercedes to see if I can keep it going another 100,000 miles."

"Do cars even run that long?" I had to admit I didn't even know the mileage on my car right now.

"They do if they're good cars and cared for well. Mrs. Fenster is at 300,000 miles and counting." He gave me a wry smile. "And that's nearly a miracle since she only drives from her house about two miles outside town to the grocery store and hair salon here," he pointed up the street a bit, "once a week."

"What? Has she owned the car for ninety years?" I laughed.

"Almost. I'm pretty sure she's a vampire."

We were both still laughing when we opened the door to the bookstore and walked straight into Walter and Stephen, my two friends from San Francisco. "Surprise," Stephen said as he hugged me and whispered, "I see you've made a friend."

I pulled back and gave Stephen a look that I hoped said, "I'm glad you're here, but don't embarrass me." Then, I hugged Walter and said, "What are you two doing here? I thought you weren't coming until the weekend."

"We couldn't wait," Stephen said as he gestured around the store. "We had to see this place. Plus, I missed you. You look good. Really good."

I grinned. Stephen had been my closest friend at work back on the West Coast, and his husband, Walter, had become a friend, too. I was giddy that they were here. "Stephen, Walter, this is Daniel. He's the town's wizard of a mechanic. We were just going to grab some coffee. Join us?"

I both desperately wanted to sit down with my friends and catch up and to sit alone with Daniel and enjoy that cup of coffee. Behind Walter's head, I could see Rocky grinning and realized that Daniel and I weren't going to have a quiet moment no matter what. I threw him a glance, "You okay if they join us?"

"Of course," he said as he bent down to let Mayhem and Taco off their leashes so that they could rush into the waiting arms of the two men who were far too excited to see them. Stephen and Walter were dog people, and these hounds knew it. The amount of squealing and wagging was extremely mutual.

Eventually, the pups took off to sniff and nap, and we headed into the café where Rocky had already prepared a large French press of coffee and put it with what had to be a secret stash of her mom's cinnamon rolls – they had certainly been secret from me – on the larger table near the front window. She gave me a wink as she headed back to the counter.

"And that, my friends, is the extraordinary Rocky Chevalier. My right-hand woman and daughter of the best baker in town."

Walter lifted a half-eaten cinnamon roll and said, "To Rocky and her mom" through a mouthful of bread.

We all joined suit, "To Rocky and her mom," and raised our cinnamon rolls high. I caught a glimpse of a customer or two headed into the café then leaving with to-go containers holding Rocky's mom's delights. The cinnamon rolls spoke for themselves.

"Now, what are you two doing here?" I asked after taking a huge swig of the perfectly strong coffee. "I don't even have your bed made yet."

"Oh goodness, woman. Don't worry about that. The real concern is if you have enough snacks for our Friday night movie binge. We have *Get Out* and *Us* to watch, you know?"

I laughed. "The house is always stocked with Cheese Doodles,

Peanut Butter M&Ms, and mini Kit Kats. Anything else is available at our local Food Lion."

"Peanut Butter M&Ms, huh? I'm in," Daniel grinned. I felt Stephen kick me under the table just before the color flushed my cheeks.

"The more the merrier," Stephen said as he winked at me. "I'm always happy to invite people over to other people's homes."

"Well, in that case," Rocky chimed in from the counter, "Count me in, too. Those movies terrified me, and it was awesome."

"Looks like we have a plan for Friday night then," I said as I stole a glance at Daniel. He was looking right at me and smiling. I blushed again and then looked away quickly. "But really, why are you guys here early?"

"Mart told us the grand opening was amazing, and we had some extra vacation time stored up. We couldn't imagine a better way to spend it than seeing our favorite bookshop owner and being by the brackish waters of the Chesapeake Bay." Stephen squeezed my hand.

"Don't let him fool you. He had to look up the body of water and the word *brackish* on the plane." Walter slipped his arm around his husband's shoulder and tugged. "Mostly, he just wanted to see you."

I felt tears leap to my eyes. "I'm so glad you're here." I grabbed Walter's hand, too, and squeezed.

We all sat quietly for a few minutes sipping our coffee, or in my case, refilling my mug. Then, Walter said, "So you're the town mechanic? I hope it's not insulting to say that I find that quaint in the best way."

Daniel laughed. "Not insulting at all. A lot of things here in St. Marin's are pretty quaint. Of course, quaint can also be a synonym for claustrophobic, but mostly, it's just nice. I grew up in a big city, so I love knowing my neighbors and their pets. It makes me feel at home, I guess."

"You grew up in a big city?" I was surprised, but I didn't know why. I knew nothing about this man, and despite popular belief held by a lot of urban dwellers, you can't spot a country person by the hay sticking out of their mouth or the gun rack in their pick-up truck. Daniel just seemed like he fit so well here, and he knew everyone.

"Yep. Chicago. But it wasn't for me. Too fast. Too many people. Too much traffic."

"You'd think that lots of cars would be good for a mechanic?" Stephen quipped.

"You would. But not for me. I like knowing the people who come to my shop. After all, a car is like a family member. It needs to be cared for well and regularly. A lot of folks in Chicago who drive are commuters, so they take their cars to garages in the suburbs. I knew I needed a smaller place."

"Makes sense," I said. "But why St. Marin's?"

"Would you believe I was sailing around the world after high school and ended up here?"

"No way." I tried to keep my mouth from hanging open.

"Oh, I didn't say I did that, just asked if you'd believe I did. I have my answer." He bumped my arm with his elbow. "Did you know that *gullible* isn't in the dictionary?"

I bumped him back and hung my head with embarrassment. I couldn't help smiling though. This guy was funny. Stephen kicked me under the table again.

"Actually, I came this way to go to Salisbury on a baseball schol-arship, but it turns out that college isn't really for me. I'm much more of a hands-on guy."

Just then, Marcus came in from the back of the store. I had totally forgotten he was here, and from the looks of him, he'd worked straight through lunch and everything. "College wasn't really for me either," he said as I handed him a tall glass of ice water. "The dorms were what got to me . . . another person I don't know all up in my stuff? Nah."

I laughed. "Yeah, I had this one roommate. She'd go to bed every night at eight and play some sort of flute music for hours at full blast. If I never hear a flute again, it'll be too soon."

Marcus laughed. "So, Ms. Beckett, we're all set. I cleaned up all the weeds and picked up a bunch of trash, too. I left a couple of piles by the corner of the building, but if you'll tell me where you want them, I'll—"

"Marcus, you have done more than enough." I headed toward the register. "Let me pay you, and you can go get a shower and head out for the rest of your day."

I saw him wince, but chalked it up to the aches and pains of hard labor. "Thanks, Mrs. Beckett. I appreciate it." He waved at everyone and then took his skateboard out the door.

"Nice kid," Stephen said.

"Hard worker, too. I hope I can give him more work soon. It's hard to find a job these days without a college degree."

"Yep, even back in my day – back in the dark ages – it was hard," Walter said. "I fought my way through college, but I hated it. It was just really not ideal for me, and I don't remember anything from any of my classes. Put me on a construction site, though, and I am in my element."

"You work construction then?" Daniel asked, and I applauded his sincerity. Walter was tall, lean, very well dressed, and had hands soft as a baby's bottom. He did not look like the stereotype of a construction worker at all.

"I did. For about fifteen years. Steel worker. But then, they figured out I was good with planning and people, so I moved into management."

"Walter is being modest. He owns one of the biggest commercial construction companies in California." I loved bragging about my friends.

"That's amazing," Daniel said with a huge smile. "There's nothing like the freedom – and the stress – of owning your own business."

"You know it," Walter smiled at Daniel, and then I felt his foot nudge mine. Any more footsie under this table, and we'd need a soccer ball.

"But you know what we need to know, right? Tell us about this person who was killed here. Are you okay?" Stephen asked.

I had almost forgotten about Stevensmith's murder. Between my ever-growing crush on Daniel and the arrival of my two friends, I had been totally distracted for thirty minutes. Remembering felt like a huge thud in my day. Still, pretending it hadn't happened wouldn't make the fact disappear, so I caught my friends up all the way through the orange piece of paper and Divina Stevensmith's strange and emphatic feelings about the color orange.

"I thought so," Stephen gave Walter a look. "She's sleuthing."

I tried to avoid eye contact, but Stephen grabbed my chin and turned my face toward him. "You can't help it, can you?"

"I'm just asking a few questions. Nothing major."

"I thought Sheriff Mason was investigating pretty seriously." Daniel's voice sounded concerned.

"Oh, he is. He is. I guess I'm just curious by nature."

"Better than naughty," Walter said almost under his breath before his eyes got wide. "Oh my goodness, did I say that out loud?"

I blushed for the kabillionth time this morning. "Anyway. No big deal. I haven't found anything anyway."

"Well, not yet, but we do need to talk to Max Davies pronto."

Daniel stood up and put his hand on my shoulder. "Be careful, Harvey, okay? This town is small. People will know if you're asking questions. There are no secrets, remember."

I liked the feel of his hand on my shoulder so much that I almost missed what he said, but then, I nodded. "I will. I think I'm being pretty discreet."

Stephen and Walter exchanged a look. "You are amazing. Kind. Generous. Easy-going. But *discreet* you are not," Stephen said. "Listen to the man. He knows this town better than you do."

I stood up, too, sad to feel Daniel's hand fall away. "Okay, okay. I'll watch myself."

"Good," all three men said at once. I laughed. "Thanks, men."

"Alright, where's your spare key? We took a red-eye, and despite this amazing coffee – thank you, Rocky! – I need a nap big time." Stephen put his arm around my shoulder.

"I'll catch up with you later, Harvey. Maybe come by when the shop closes up to walk you home." Daniel said as he stood.

"Oh, you don't—"

52

"That's perfect. You can just walk Harvey home if that suits," Walter said.

I tried to keep my eyes in my head as my friends told someone they barely knew what to do.

"We are going to be cooking a fine dinner, so join us tonight," Walter continued. "I hear the seafood is amazing here." He looked at me. "Don't worry, Miss 'I Hate Seafood,' I have an amazing gourmet burger in mind for you."

"Sounds good to me." Daniel whistled and Taco came running. Well, galumphing might be a more accurate description. "I'll see you soon, Harvey."

The bell rang, and the man and his dog slipped out the front door.

"Harvey! That man likes you." Stephen was anything but quiet, and I was pleased, for once, that we didn't have any customers in the shop at the moment. "And from the flush on your cheeks, I'd say you like him too."

"Love is in the air," Walter chimed in.

"You two need to stop. I barely know the man."

"Since when did that matter? I knew I wanted to marry Walter on our first date. And we were engaged in three months. When you know, you know."

"Well, I don't know anything, so you two go on and get a nap. I'm looking forward to my burger." I took each man by an arm and walked them to the door. "I'm so glad you're here, guys. Really. You've made my week. Thank you for coming."

"We wouldn't have missed it. A friend, a murder, and a little romance. It's like a movie right here in this little shop." Stephen gave me a kiss on the cheek and then they headed to my house.

I headed to the counter, sat down, and put my face on the cool wood. Two evenings with Daniel in one week. I couldn't stop smiling.

Chapter Six

The rest of the afternoon went by uneventfully. A steady stream of customers, including a mom of a young boy who wanted books that taught him to be compassionate. I could have spent all afternoon recommending titles to her, but when she settled on *The Quiltmaker's Gift*, one of my favorites, I was delighted. The illustrations alone made that book worth owning. But the story was sweet and generous, too. I thought her son would love it.

At exactly seven, Rocky and I turned off the lights and headed out the door. In the past few days, I'd developed the habit of double-checking the alarmed bar I'd had installed on the back door after Stevensmith's murder, and tonight, I triple-checked it. I didn't want anything – especially a break-in – to interrupt our dinner tonight. I tried to tell myself that it was because my friends were in town, but mostly, it was a certain dark-haired man and his Basset Hound I could see waiting on the sidewalk.

Daniel and I strolled in silence for a couple of blocks, and I noted how comfortable I felt. Again. This felt too easy, but maybe that was the way of things that were actually mutual. I hadn't had much luck with that in my marriage, so I wouldn't know.

As we turned off Main Street, Daniel said, "So, Walter and Stephen, I like them."

I grinned. "I like them, too. They're good people, and they've been amazing friends to me." While we walked the last few blocks to my house, I told him about the time Walter had come to pick me up when my tire had blown in an Oakland parking lot at about two a.m. My ex-husband hadn't answered his phone, and I was at a loss. The other people who had attended the concert with me were leaving steadily, and I was getting more and more nervous waiting in the lot for a taxi. But then, Walter, after getting a text from Stephen who was in Seattle but who I'd texted just for company while I waited for my cab, rolled up and got me. He drove me home, making jokes all the way. I felt embarrassed, but I also felt so grateful. "They really are amazing."

"I can tell," Daniel said as we walked up to my house. All the lights were on, and I could see Mart dancing by the kitchen island. It was going to be a good night.

Sure enough, when we opened the door, a puff of warm, garlic-scented air engulfed us, and the sounds of Little Big Town spilled out. Neither Mart nor I were country music fans, but there was just something about that group's harmonies that made us happy. Apparently, Walter and Stephen felt the same way because when I turned the corner from the foyer into the kitchen, they were both singing into wooden spoons . . . and they weren't bad either.

"Nice harmony, guys," I said as I draped the scarf Mart had crocheted me during her "yarn phase" of 2016. That year, she had made everyone we knew scarves and had gotten strangely invested in Maggie Sefton's knitting mysteries. She even made me take a road trip to Fort Collins so we could visit the town that the books were set in. When she saw the yarn shop that inspired the theme for the books, she had teared up. It was a tender year for both of us. I was happy that 2017 was the year of baked goods and thrillers. It made for a little less wool and a few more scary movies accompanied by macaroons.

"Daniel, glad you're here," Walter said as he headed toward my fridge. "Beer or wine?"

"Beer, please."

"You got it. Light or dark?"

"Light." Walter popped the cap off a Corona and handed it to Daniel.

I made my way to the fridge and opened it up. When I'd left that morning, we'd had half a loaf of bread, some really good gouda, leftover boxed mac and cheese, and eighteen jars of pickles. Now, the fridge was jammed with fresh herbs in glasses of water, a whole shelf of fresh produce, and more wine and beer than I could count. The guys had been shopping.

I poured a glass of Chateau St. Jean Chardonnay and turned to Stephen. "You remembered."

"How could I forget? You gush about that place all the time. Plus, it has that quirky name that seems French but is really just super-American. Chateau St. Jean," he looked at Daniel, "like denim or genetics, not the French man's name. Weird, right?"

"Definitely weird." Daniel winked at me as he took a sip of his beer, and I felt my knees give a little.

Mart gave me the signal – meaning, she grabbed my hand and dragged me into my bedroom – and said, "Daniel is here!"

I tried to play it cool. "Yes, I know. I brought him." But then, I broke down and giggled. "I know."

"Okay, okay. We're so cool." She let out a long breath. "And he winked at you." She giggled this time. "Okay, cool, cool." She grabbed my hand and dragged me back. We were anything but subtle in our silliness, but none of the guys seemed to mind.

Mayhem and Taco had passed out on the rug by the fireplace, and Aslan was tentatively getting comfy on the chair near the heat but not too near the dogs. It was clear that she resented the dogs taking *her* space, but her sense of self-preservation kept her near her escape route, the bookshelf.

Soon, Walter and Stephen served us the most glorious-smelling seafood and a burger so big that I needed two hands to hold it, and we all tucked in. The food was amazing, and I kept looking around the table with sheer delight. These were my people, and they were here for me. Even Daniel . . . or at least I hoped Daniel was going to be one of my people. I tried not to think *my person*.

As we all finished up our meals and I considered undoing the button on my jeans, Mart smacked a hand on the table and said, "I totally forgot to tell you," she looked at me, "but I stopped at the farmer's market today to see Eleanor about some centerpieces for our big gala in a couple of weeks. And as I walked in, the sheriff was leaving. Eleanor looked like death warmed over. Her hands were shaking."

"Oh my goodness. Did she say what happened?" I leaned forward, my hands gripping the table edge. My mind had immediately gone to that little corner of paper and the origami flowers Eleanor had in the window.

"She didn't give me all the details – I think she was embarrassed – but she said Sheriff Mason had been asking her questions about Stevensmith and her death. I got the impression she had just been questioned, maybe as a suspect."

Walter said, "Ooh, now this is getting good. Is she a suspect?" He looked at me.

Part of me wanted to say, "How should I know?" but the honest part of me nodded. "I think maybe she is." I told them about the flowers in the window of her shop, and a tiny glimmer of something important passed behind my eyes too quickly for me to catch it. I made a mental note to come back to that idea.

"So now we have three suspects? Max Davies, Divina Stevensmith, and Eleanor Heron," Mart said with a bit of mischief in her tone. "The plot thickens."

I caught Stephen and Daniel exchanging a worried look and didn't know whether to be put out or pleased that everyone was bonding so well. "What?!" I said to the pair.

I saw a little pink moved into Daniel's cheeks as he avoided looking me in the eye. Stephen couldn't get off so easy though as I grabbed his cheeks and made him look at me, just as he'd done to me in the café earlier. "What?!"

"Just last time you snooped into a murder . . . "

"Wait, what happened last time? There was a last time?" Daniel looked from me to Stephen and back to me again.

I let out a hard sigh. "Yes, and it all ended fine."

"True. But you almost died." Stephen could not keep his mouth shut.

"That may be a bit of an exaggeration. But anyway, that's another story for another time." I was desperate to avoid any talk of my life back in San Francisco. Too much baggage there to foist on a guy I could really like. I didn't want to scare him off. "We have a murder here, now, and it happened in my store. That makes it personal."

"Now, there's a question," Walter said as he got up to grab the pot of decaf coffee. "Do you think the person planned the murder for your store? "

"No, definitely not. Stevensmith wasn't hit in my store. She just came to hide there."

Stephen took a long sip of his scalding hot coffee and asked, "But did she come to die in your store on purpose?"

I shuddered. "I certainly hope not." I looked down at the hand-thrown coffee mug that I'd picked up in a little pottery studio when Mart and I had taken a weekend trip to the Shenandoah National Park over the winter. "But I hadn't thought of that. Is that possible? Can someone with a serious head injury think that clearly to pick a specific place to die?"

Daniel put his hand over mine, and I felt all the blood rush to my face. It didn't help that Mart, Walter, and Stephen all kicked my leg at the same moment. "I expect she just happened to be close by, saw the back door, and hid anywhere she could. She probably didn't even know where she was."

I resisted the urge to pull my hand away from Daniel's. I loved the feel of it there, but I didn't love the way my friends were ogling our hands. I stayed still and smiled at him. "Thanks. I expect you're right." I gave his fingers a little squeeze and then slid my hand into my lap. "That does beg the question, though. Where did she get attacked?"

Mart was up before I finished my exhale following my question. "Let's go find out," she said as she handed me my scarf.

"What?" I looked down at the blue knitted band and back at my friend. "What?! No. We aren't going to try to find where the murder happened. Not at nine o'clock at night. No."

But I could see that Walter had already slid on his leather bomber jacket, and Stephen was easing his chair back from the table. Only Daniel and I were still sitting there, and even he looked like he wanted to get up.

"I see I have no say here. Alright, let's go." I wrapped the scarf around my neck and pulled on my peacoat. We gave Mayhem and Taco the hamburger that Stephen and Walter had cooked just for them and headed toward the door. I was bringing up the rear so I could lock the door behind us, but Daniel lingered back and turned to me just as I reached the door

"I'm in for whatever adventure this is, but I want you to be careful, okay?" His eyes were soft, and the gentleness of his voice almost brought me to tears.

"Okay. I will." I smiled. "I'm glad you're here."

Then, he took my hand and squeezed as we went out the door.

The night was crisp and clear. In our part of town, the streetlights were few and far between, so we could see thousands of stars overhead. The cold air and the starshine made us all a little playful as we skipped and laughed our way back to Main Street. Daniel and I opened the front door and disarmed the alarm at the back of the shop while Stephen, Walter, and Mart headed around back from the outside to take a look at the parking lot. We were just about through the store when I heard Mart exclaim, "Oh no!"

I ran the last few steps only to find the back door wide open, the security bar popped free from the door jamb.

"Holy crap," Walter said. "It looks like a bear tried to take your door off."

Daniel knelt down and looked closely at the door jamb. "Only if a bear uses a crow bar."

"A crow bar?" I knelt down and looked. Sure enough, there were scraps and dents in the metal door frame. Someone had pried the door open and forced the security bar loose.

"Clearly, someone desperately needed a copy of John Grisham's new book immediately," Stephen said wryly. Then, he looked at me and said, "You have insurance. It'll cover this."

I nodded. "It will, but why would someone break into my bookstore? And why didn't the alarm go off?"

"That's an easy one," Mart said, holding up some wires that had been pulled out of a box on the wall.

"Seriously? The alarm company put the junction box for your system on the outside of the building?" Daniel sounded angry. "Tomorrow, I'll talk with them. Tonight, let's just get this secure and call the sheriff."

I couldn't help but smile when he looked at me and said, "I mean, if that's okay with you, Harvey. It's your shop. This just makes me so mad."

"I think that's a good plan. But while we're back here, we might as well do what we came to do." I tried to sound confident because I really did want to look around, but I could feel my heart at the back of my throat.

Stephen acted as if he was holding a magnifying glass up to his eye. "I'm on the hunt for clues."

"Okay, you guys look around. I'll go inside and call the sheriff." I started for the door, but Walter grabbed my arm.

"Maybe you should stay out here. We don't know that whoever did this is gone." Walter said as he handed me his cell phone. I made the call, and then we all stood close together in the back parking lot until Sheriff Mason arrived in a cruiser with Deputy Williams in another car close behind him.

We told him what we'd found, and the deputy took some photos and then dusted for prints. Meanwhile, the sheriff took us all inside and had me look for anything that was missing. "I know you may not notice if a particular book is gone—"

Mart interrupted him. "Oh, Harvey will notice."

I nodded. "I straighten the shelves every night. I should be able to see any gaps." I took a quick lap around the small shop, but I didn't notice any books missing. I was just heading back to the café to let the sheriff know when I saw that the storeroom door was ajar. I was certain I'd shut it when I closed the store.

I got Daniel's attention, and he and the sheriff came over. I pointed at the door.

Mason looked at the door and then back at me. "Again?" He let out a heavy sigh and used his boot to push open the door.

The lights were on, but other than that – I always turned them off; I couldn't afford any extra pennies on the electric bill – nothing looked out of place. "Looks fine," I said when the sheriff looked my way again.

"Okay. Humor me, though, and take a walk around." He looked at Daniel. "You'll stay with her?"

"Of course," Daniel said with a firm nod.

I had to duck behind a stack of boxes to hide my grin, and when I did, I saw a small puddle of water. I looked up to be sure the ceiling wasn't leaking and breathed a sigh of relief when I didn't see any drops. Roof leaks are expensive. "Daniel, would you mind taking a look?"

He came over from the door, and when I pointed, he laid a gentle hand on my back as he bent down to study the water. I felt my heartbeat quicken.

"Water?"

"Yeah, but not from the roof I don't think."

"Weird." He looked up, too. "Yeah, I don't see any sign of water up there."

"Maybe from someone's shoes or something?"

"Could be. But it's not raining, so I don't know."

He gave me a sideways grin. "Maybe it's like that old riddle, and it was an icicle and now the murder weapon has melted."

He chuckled. "If Stevensmith had been stabbed, I might think you were onto something." He winked. "That combined with the fact that it's far too warm for icicles makes me question your theory."

I smiled. "Way to crush a girl's dreams."

"Sometimes the truth hurts." He bent down and put a finger in the water and then touched the tip of his finger to his tongue. I would have been grossed out if I hadn't thought about doing the same thing. "Just water," he said.

"So odd."

He nodded, and we headed out of the storeroom, turning off the light and closing the door behind us. We made our way to the front of the store, where the sheriff and our friends waited. "Alright, so we'll patrol through overnight and come take a closer look at things in the morning." Until then, we've put a big old padlock on the back door – your insurance should cover the repairs for that, too, Harvey – to keep it secure. Just be sure to call your alarm company first thing since you won't have a second egress if there's a fire."

"Oh Lord, please, let's hope we don't also add a fire to a murder and a break-in," Mart said. "I'll come in tomorrow and handle that stuff." She pulled me close in a side-armed hug.

"And we're here, too, so we'll help in the shop and keep an eye out for suspicious folks, too." Stephen winked at the sheriff.

"You have good friends, Harvey."

"I do. Thanks, Sheriff."

"Ready to lock up?" Mason held the door open for everyone but Mart and me. I wanted to do a last pass through the store, be sure everything was closed up tight The two of us went to the back door and double checked the lock. Then, I made sure some lights were on in both the shop and the café. As we headed toward the front door, Mart stopped me with a hand on my arm. "We did find that," she pointed to the right, "but I don't know if it's anything. So I wanted you to see it just in case it's nothing."

Behind the free-standing shelf that held biographies and memoirs, she had propped up a thin umbrella with a long, black handle. "Mart, we need to tell the sheriff—"

"We will, tomorrow."

I could see Daniel's face under the street lamp outside, and he seemed a little nervous. "Tonight, we've had enough." She gave me a little shove toward the door. "Let's go."

I started to hesitate, but the store was locked up tight, and I knew Williams would be stopping by on patrol. I decided I could call the sheriff first thing, even before the alarm company.

We scooted out, and the little bell above the door was still ringing as I locked it.

The next morning, I had this awful feeling that the umbrella was going to be gone and I had lost valuable evidence for the investigation, so I gobbled down a bowl of cereal and sprinted with Mayhem to the shop before the sun was even up all the way.

When I spun around the corner of the biography shelf, I was relieved to see the umbrella still there, just as it had been. I led Mayhem around the store just to be sure we were all clear and checked the lock at the back. Everything was as it should be, well, except for the fact that someone had been murdered in my shop and there'd been a break-in. Otherwise, everything was fine.

I grabbed a plastic bag from under the counter and went to scoop up the umbrella. I didn't know that there was any value in not leaving my fingerprints – after all, Mart had been carrying the thing in her bare hands – but figured better safe than sorry. As I picked it up, I noticed a small puddle on the wooden floor beneath where it had stood. I glanced at the umbrella and back at the puddle. For the most part, the umbrella itself was dry, but down in the tip, I could see little glistens of water droplets. *This* was the source of the puddle in the storeroom, I was sure of it.

The sheriff needed to know, and I had delayed long enough. I gave the sheriff's office a ring, and the person on duty said he'd be over shortly. In the meantime, I had some puzzling to do. The umbrella was what the person had broken in to get, clearly, but then why had they dropped it out back? And why was it wet?

I had an inkling of the first answer – from the description it seemed likely this was the murder weapon. The thin, cylindrical handle was made of some sort of metal coated in a thin cover of what felt like black rubber that reminded me of the spray stuff a lot of the folks with pick-up trucks used to protect their beds from scratches. Maybe the sheriff had found traces of that rubber in Stevensmith's wound or maybe they had done a mold of the injury . . . I stopped myself before I let my fascination with TV dramas lead me too far into things I didn't really want to think about.

I had just finished making a pot of coffee in the café when I heard a knock at the door and saw the sheriff waving a small, white bag in front of his face. I smiled – next to Rocky's Mom's cinnamon rolls, the sausage-egg-and-cheese biscuits from the gas station up the road were the best breakfast in town. I felt my stomach rumble – cereal was just a teaser of a breakfast.

"Thought you might need fortification," the sheriff said as I unlocked the door. "Now, where's this mysterious item you found in your snooping?"

I blushed. "We were just curious," I said as I led us to the table at the front of the café.

"You know what happened to the cat?"

I shivered. I did know. "It's right here," I said and gestured to the umbrella I'd propped against the table. "I think it's what left a puddle in the storeroom. It left another where Mart set it last night."

The sheriff picked up the umbrella in his gloveless hands, confirming my guess that fingerprints were a moot point, and looked up at me. "Smart move not to call me back last night. I imagine whoever cared enough to break in accidentally dropped this when you and your friends showed up. It's best they not know we recovered it."

"A bit of luck, that. I was just sleepy and figured you were, too. "

"Courtesy and good rest will carry you a long way in this world," the sheriff said through a mouthful of biscuit. "What puzzles me is the water. You're sure this wasn't here before?"

I took a minute to think about the storeroom over the last few days. "I don't think so, but I can't be totally sure. I've been in and out of there several times, of course, but always in a hurry or with my arms full. Not sure I would have noticed it behind the boxes where it seems like it was. We should ask Rocky. Her café supplies are in there, too."

"*I* will ask Rocky, Ms. Super Sleuth. Leave the police work to me, okay?"

I tilted my head and said, "Sure," with a wide grin.

"It's like talking to a brick wall," the sheriff muttered with a small smile. "I expect you know this is probably the murder weapon, right?"

"I wondered. Right shape?"

"Looks like it. Heavy enough, too," he said as he dropped the handle into his hand a couple of times. "And it's long, so someone smaller could get a lot of leverage if they swung it like a bat."

I cringed. The image of that happening in my storeroom made me a little queasy. "So a woman isn't out of the question."

"Nope. Not at all."

I sighed. I didn't like the idea of anyone murdering anyone, but a woman committing murder felt a little worse to me than if a man had done it, like a strike against the sisterhood or something.

"Any news on that orange paper?" I asked with what I felt like was a casual air.

The sheriff was on to me, though. "You mean besides the flowers at Heron's Farm Stand, the art in Divina's studio, and the old menus from Chez Cuisine."

I laughed. "Right. Besides that?"

"Nope, Ms. Super Sleuth, I believe you have found our best leads there, but nothing has turned up yet."

I nodded as he stood and took the umbrella. "Mind if I duck out the back? I'd rather not have all of town see me carrying an umbrella on a perfectly sunny day."

I looked out the window and realized the sun was up, and it was gorgeous, the kind of spring morning that made me want to plant a million flowers. "Sure thing. Need me to unlock it."

"Nope, got my key right here." I'd been grateful when he'd told me he kept a spare key to the padlock, just in case. It felt like I had back-up.

"Be wise, okay, Harvey? All joking aside. Someone is very invested," he gestured toward the shop's back door, "in not being caught. Don't go riling folks up, okay?"

I nodded. I knew he was right. I needed to be more discreet . . . but just how is one discreet in a town where everyone knows everyone and everyone's business?

I spent the next couple of hours ordering books and checking the alphabetization on the shelves, so by the time Mart and Rocky arrived a little before ten, I felt totally calm. One of the reasons I had wanted to open this store was that it was tangible in ways that my previous job as a fundraiser for nonprofits hadn't been. For one, I could see what I was selling. I loved e-books, too, but there was nothing like a physical book to soothe my soul. I was looking into selling e-books through our shop website, too, but I knew I wanted to focus most of my time – and money – on the print copies that filled these shelves.

Plus shelving – it was like meditation to me. Give me a big library cart full of picture books and leave me to it . . . I'll be calm and rested by day's end. Today, though, I didn't have a cart of books to shelve, and my frazzled nerves sure could have used them.

Mart wasted no time calling the insurance and alarm companies about getting the alarm system and door repaired. She gave me a wink as I turned on the final banks of lights and flipped on the cute neon sign that featured Mayhem with her head resting on a few books below the word *Open*. Stephen and Walter had commissioned that for me, and it was still my favorite moment of the morning – to pull the little chain and light up that sign.

Woody came by just as I was heading to the café for my morning latte, so I got him one, too, and assured him that everything was fine and that we hadn't been robbed. The grapevine was already going strong.

"Okay, Harvey," he said. "I'm not going to ask any more questions then. I get the sense that it's best to leave things where they lie.

But you call me if you need anything." He looked at me seriously. "I mean that."

Spontaneously, I gave him a hug, and he squeezed me tight before heading to the front door with his to-go cup.

I was heading back to the register with a fresh latte for me and one for Mart when I heard the bell ring and saw two older women, one white and one Asian, come in the store and head right for the fiction section. In my shop, I didn't divide out genre fiction – horror, mystery, fantasy – from literary fiction like some stores did. Books were books, and I wanted everybody to get equal billing. No second-class books here. I couldn't wait to see what they picked up – at least I hoped they picked something up.

"Walter and Stephen still asleep?" I asked as I handed Mart her mug.

She nodded while she took a long, smooth sip. "Jet lag."

"Jet lag and wine," I said with a smile.

"The best combo." Mart and I clinked our white, ceramic mugs. "Alarm company will be over later this morning, and the insurance process is started. I'll keep an eye out for the tech when they arrive."

I thanked my best friend and caught her up on my conversation with the sheriff until the two customers arrived at the counter with a few books each. I complimented their choices – the new Rene Denfeld, an Alice Hoffman title, Jesmyn Ward's latest, my favorite novel ever, *Who Fears Death* by Nnedi Okorafor, and a fun YA fantasy novel called *Supernatural Reform School*. I liked their eclectic taste and told them so, then glowed when they said they'd definitely be back and would tell their friends over in Annapolis about the shop.

Before the bell could even stop ringing over the front door, Mart was jumping up and down and holding my hands. "You know who that was, right?"

I looked at the door and then back at my friend. "Who? One of those women?"

"Not just one of those women. Michiko Kakutani – the book reviewer for the *New York Times*."

"Oh," I knew I was supposed to be impressed, but I didn't know why. "She's a big deal, I guess?"

Mart slapped a palm to her forehead. "You are impossible. She's the biggest deal. If she mentions your bookstore anywhere, it'll be huge."

"Well, then I hope she tells all her friends."

Mart shook her head and headed to the café for a latte refill. A few moments later, I heard Rocky shout, "Michiko Kakutani was here?" Guess she *was* a big deal.

While I was still googling Kakutani and considering what residual boon her visit to the shop might be, I caught a glimpse of Marcus riding down the sidewalk and rushed out to catch him. "Marcus!" I called his name down the street, but he didn't slow. So I jogged – something I try to avoid doing unless being chased – and shouted more loudly. This time he stopped and pulled an ear bud out of his ear before turning back toward me.

"Oh, hi Ms. Beckett. I'm sorry. I didn't hear you. You okay?"

I was out of breath, and I imagined my face was flushed since even climbing a flight of stairs could bring the color to my cheeks. I made a commitment to do a little more than stroll the neighborhood with Mayhem over the next couple of months. "Yes, I'm fine. Sorry. Just wanted to catch you and see if you might have time to do a bit more work for me."

He smiled. "Oh yeah, I'd be happy to. What do you need?"

"Well, someone broke into my shop, and I need a little help fixing the door and doing some painting. Is that something you'd be comfortable doing?"

"Absolutely." He sounded eager, almost excited, and I wondered, again, about his story. "When do you need me?"

"When are you free?"

He paused and a sad look passed over his face, but then he met my gaze again and said, "Anytime, really. I'm, uh, between projects right now."

"Alrighty then. This afternoon? Come by about noon, and I'll hook you up with a sandwich, too. It's the least I could do for bringing you on so suddenly."

His smile grew. "Sounds like a plan. See you soon."

I turned back to the shop and wondered how I might get Marcus to tell me about himself. There was something I didn't know about that young man, and it felt like it might be important for me to know it.

———

Stephen and Walter came in about eleven looking well-rested and ready to work, and since Mart was handling alarm repairs and the insurance and Marcus was going to do the clean-up and painting on the door, I asked if they could help me by sorting the stock room. It had been creeping me out that everything was still in the same place as when Stevensmith had been killed, and the sheriff said I could go ahead and move things.

The guys were oddly enthused by the idea. Walter asked, "So do you want everything organized by color or alphabet?"

I cringed. "By alphabet. I've never understood bookshelves organized by color. I mean they look pretty, but I would never be able to find anything."

Stephen nodded, but Walter said, "You verbal people will never get us visual folks. I never remember who wrote a book, but I can tell you what the cover looked like in perfect detail."

"He can," Stephen agreed, "but since most of the folks will not know these books and, thus, can't know the covers, I think it's best to follow the expert's lead here." He gave me a wink, and they headed to the back.

I spent the next hour paying bills and trying to wrangle my budget. I was doing okay, but not as well as I'd dreamed we might. Maybe that Kakutani person's visit would be a little burst of press? Fingers crossed.

I was just about to head over to the café and see what Rocky might be able to make Marcus for lunch when the bell rang, and I looked over to see Taco making a beeline for a table of customers that included a toddler who was gladly sharing his scone with Mayhem. Taco was not about to be left out of that action.

I followed his trail back toward the door and saw Daniel. He waved and headed over. "Mart said you had help today, so I wondered if I could steal you for the afternoon?"

I looked toward the back of the store where Mart, Stephen, and Walter were huddled together watching. I took a quick peek to be sure they didn't have a tub of popcorn for their feature film.

"Um, sure," I said turning back to Daniel. "Looks like things here are under control. Let me just grab my coat."

I walked briskly toward my friends, who didn't even have the decency to scatter and pretend they hadn't been watching, and hissed as I walked by, "You three are ridiculous. Mart, you told him to come by? What is this, junior high?"

"Oh no, woman, this is big girl romance. I'm just moving things along. But if you want me to ask him if he likes you later . . . "

I gave her a death glare. "Marcus will be here shortly. I told him I'd feed him, and then he's going to repair the door and paint. Give him a bit of cash from the register to get what he needs next door." Having a hardware store as your neighbor is never a bad thing.

"Yes, Ma'am," Mart said with a click of her heels and a smirk. "Now, your date is waiting."

I shot her another scowl as I rushed back by and then grinned when I saw Daniel patiently waiting. "Taco can stay here if you want." I looked over at the long, low dog. "Looks like he and Mayhem are content." Both dogs had found their way onto the very large dog bed I'd placed on the center of the stage in the café and were snoozing butt to butt.

"Oh, a dog's life," Daniel said.

"You can say that again."

We headed out the door and turned down Main Street. "Tacos okay?" Daniel asked as we sauntered along. The weather was perfect, and I was content to let my meddling friends manage the store all day.

"Sounds great. And actually, if you're up for it, I have a little research I need to do at the library after."

"Research, huh? Why do I think this isn't book research?"

I gave him a sly smile and slipped my hand onto his arm. He

immediately covered my fingers with his own, and I felt my heart kick.

After a completely delightful meal of some of the best tacos I've ever eaten – I was pretty sure they'd inspired Daniel's dog's name – and a lovely chat on a park bench while we ate our food truck meal, I coaxed Daniel over to the beautiful brick library a block off Main Street. "I guess the library is pretty new, huh?"

"Yeah, the old one had been in a storefront on Main Street, but the town decided to move it and give that space to more tourist-friendly businesses. Not many out-of-towners use the local library."

"That makes sense. And this is gorgeous," I said as we walked into a beautiful, light-filled atrium where the circulation desk sat surrounded by potted plants. "I could work here."

"What?! Work for the competition? Never?!" Daniel said with mock awe.

I laughed. "Actually, I don't think of the library as competition, more as camaraderie on the quest to help people find books they love."

Daniel leaned over and kissed me on the cheek. "I like that," he said. "Now, what are we here for?"

It took me a while to get my words back after that show of affection, but I eventually stammered that I wanted to look at the old newspapers. Then I said I first needed to use the restroom and rushed off to splash my face with cold water.

When I came back, Daniel did a wide sweep with his arm and pointed toward the back of the building. "To the microfilm, my lady."

I giggled. "Thank goodness they're on microfilm. I love print as much as anybody, but I'm glad we don't have to sort through years of paper."

The microfilm machines were as new as the building, and with a little guidance from the librarian, we found the older issues of the *St.*

Marin's Courier and got the first reel loaded to the machine. As I started to scroll, Daniel asked, "So what are we looking for?"

"Well, I was wondering if what got Stevensmith killed was something in one of her articles."

"Ah, I see. So we're looking for motive then?"

I looked at him out of the corner of my eye and could see his exaggerated expression of serious interest. "Yes, we're looking for motive."

"So we're just ignoring Sheriff Mason's caution?"

"What caution?" I tried to act blissfully ignorant.

"The one he shared with me after he came to see you at the store this morning."

I harrumphed. "Does no one think I can manage my own life? First Mart, and now the sheriff?"

Daniel bumped my shoulder. "He's just concerned and knew I would be, too. I told him I'd keep you close, but that I didn't think I could stop a force of your nature."

I wanted to be annoyed, to be frustrated that everyone was speaking to people about me, but I couldn't be. It just felt so nice to have people care . . . to have Daniel care.

"Alright," I let out a long sigh. "I'll be careful. Not tell anyone what I'm doing." I looked around the library to see no one was in this section. "Fair enough?"

"Fair enough if you let me help."

"You'll need your own machine."

"Oh, no I won't. I'm staying right here. The sheriff said to keep you close."

I was going to have to go splash my face again if this kept up. "I can live with that. Let's get going."

The Courier was a tiny paper, but Stevensmith had been there a long time – twelve or thirteen years – and in a small paper, most of the articles had her byline. The majority were run-of-the-mill stuff – coverage of car accidents or local events. But the reporter also had a habit of making statements – like the ones she said to me – that came off as just plain mean-spirited. If I had wagered a guess, I'd say Stevensmith was a woman who had been hurt and was taking out her pain on everyone else.

Eventually, we caught up to where the microfilm ended, having compiled a stack of fifteen to twenty pages worth of articles where Stevensmith was criticizing someone or something. But we still had the last four years of newspapers to cover online. We headed to a bank of computers, and I secretly hoped that Daniel would want to work on the same screen with me again. When he pulled another chair into the cubicle I chose, I smiled.

We scanned quickly through the last three and a half years – it was so much easier to read newspaper on a computer screen than on microfilm – and eventually came into this year. I was almost out of weekly issues when I came upon a long article about the Harriet Tubman Festival from the weekend before. Most of the article was just normal stuff – an interview with the founder, a brief biography on Tubman, some highlights of the events around town – but at the bottom of the front page, where the article was featured, Stevensmith had written:

While this festival is a good tourist event for St. Marin's, it's a shame it's for such an over-lauded person. Sure, Tubman survived slavery, but she was not the only one. Plus, wise students of history will take note that Tubman's escapades on the Underground Railroad were actually illegal, acts of theft of property. Perhaps we should be revising our history to remember her as the criminal she was rather than as a hero.

As I read those words, I gasped. Stevensmith had gone after a long-dead woman who had saved countless people from the horrors of slavery. "I can't even believe someone would say that . . . about Harriet Tubman."

"Too bad Harriet Tubman's ghost doesn't carry that gun she owned," Daniel said quietly.

"I hear that. Why would someone say such awful things?"

Daniel just shook his head while I pressed print.

As we walked back to the shop so I could close up for the night, I asked, "Want to come over tonight and help me piece together the suspect list?"

Daniel took my hand and squeezed it. "I wish I could, but I have a standing date on Thursday nights."

"Oh." A date, huh? I didn't like the sound of that.

"With the dog groomer." Daniel squeezed my hand again. "I have to get Taco's nails trimmed once a week or it sounds like someone is dropping tacks all over the floor whenever he walks. It's his weekly Puppy-Cure."

I laughed. "Oh my. I didn't take you as one to port your pooch to the doggy spa."

"There's a lot you don't know about me, yet, Harvey Beckett. A whole lot." He winked.

Chapter Seven

That night, after I'd filled Mart, Stephen, and Walter in on my lunch with Daniel in the excruciating detail that they demanded, the four of us clambered down to the floor around our coffee table and started reading the articles Daniel and I had copied. We'd each read an article and highlight anything that felt "murder-worthy" with our assigned color – I had insisted I have blue because it was my favorite – and then pass it on.

The task was made incessantly more difficult by Aslan's persistent laying on each stack of paper in succession. Someone new to cats might have tried to relocate her, but I was a seasoned cat owner and knew that such tactics only deepened feline resolve. So we simply slid the paper out from under her when we needed it and allowed her to place her girth on the next stack.

After an hour or so, we'd ended up with four articles that felt vicious enough to warrant murder. One was the review that Max Davies was obviously so bitter about, one was the Tubman article. The third was a note about a local tractor show that Stevensmith had called "degenerate" while also describing the people who brought their tractors as "hillbillies who wouldn't know their arses from their exhaust." And the final article insulted a high school English teacher who had spent thousands of her own dollars buying books for a Little Free Library on campus so that the students could have easy access to reading material. The Library had been vandalized, and the act had broken the teacher down to tears, which prompted Stevensmith to say she was a weak-hearted woman who should know better than to do more than was required in her government job.

"This woman was a piece of work," Stephen said when he'd read the last article. "I kind of want to kill her myself."

"Daniel and I said the same thing. She was a really horrible person." I couldn't believe someone would put such awful things in print.

The doorbell rang, and I jumped up with my wallet to pay for our pizza. We'd been so engrossed in our research that we'd all forgotten to eat.

When I opened the door, I was surprised to see Cate and Lucas at the door, pizza box in hand. "You were *not* the pizza delivery people I was expecting."

"No?" Cate grinned. "We were coming by to see your friends – did they mention that we met when we stopped by the shop earlier today while you were on your date," she winked, and I shook my head, "and caught the delivery gal at the end of the walk. Our treat." She handed me the piping hot box.

"Well, thanks. Come in and join us. Plenty for everyone." I gestured toward the door and followed them up the walk.

Just as we were about to head in, Cate turned and whispered. "Daniel was practically glowing when I went in to get my oil changed just before he closed. Must have been some date."

"It wasn't really a date," I said, but I couldn't help but smile.

"Uh-huh, I see that." Cate gave me a wink and went on inside.

After we all had slices of super-greasy, super-perfect pizza, I caught Cate and Lucas up on what we'd found in the articles. "I stopped reading her stuff a long time ago. Made me too angry, especially when she went after the museum." Cate's jaw was set. "No one messes with my man."

"Oh yeah, that article was brutal . . . and Stevensmith was wrong—you aren't a bit bloated, if you don't mind me saying, Lucas," Stephen said. "What was her deal?"

"No one really knew, and lots of folks tried to get her let go from the paper," Lucas said. "But her articles sold subscriptions. A lot of the people who summer here kept a subscription online just so they could see who Stevensmith would slam next. A classic case of sensational journalism if ever there was one."

I took another slice of pizza and proceeded to peel the cheese off and eat it with my fingers while I pondered. "But if everyone knew she was hateful, why would it still make someone mad? I mean, she was pretty much pissing off people who knew better than to read what she said anyway, right?"

"True," Cate said, "but people still got mad. Anytime someone says something demeaning about you, it stings, even if you know you shouldn't take it personally."

I thought of Max Davies and how bitter he still was about that review from five years ago. She'd been pretty hard on Elle Heron, too. And that poor English teacher. Cate was right. Lots of people had a reason to dislike Stevensmith. "But does it sting badly enough to kill her? I mean you have to be either hopping mad or really angry for a really long time to commit a murder, don't you?"

"I'd think so," Walter said as he got up to refill everyone's glasses with Pepsi. The only drink that befits great pizza is Pepsi, and I was glad to see my friends all agreed. "But then, I've never committed murder."

The room got quiet for a while, and then Mart said, "Okay, who's up for Apples to Apples?"

Everyone looked at her like she'd just sprouted a second head until she said, "The game. You don't know it? I thought it might be fun to play since we're all here anyway."

"I'd be up for a round or two," Cate said.

"It's not like we're going to solve this murder tonight, anyway," I said as I grabbed wine glasses and two bottles of pinot noir. Pepsi for pizza, red wine for after.

"I'm pretty sure the sheriff would prefer you not try to solve anything, my dear," Stephen said as he poured himself a large glass and resumed his seat on the floor. "But I also expect he knows, by now, that his preferences and your desires might not align."

I kicked him under the table and smiled. He was right.

The next day, the shop was busy from the minute we opened until we closed at seven. Michiko Kakutani had indeed mentioned the shop on Twitter and included a photo of the storefront, and that, coupled with what Cate told me were the usual beginnings of the tourist season, meant we had an amazing day of sales.

I was grateful . . . for the sales, but also for the distraction because, of course, tonight Daniel was coming over for movie night. If the shop had been slow, I would have probably gnawed my fingers to the first joint. As it was, I simply had a very short, very ragged manicure.

When we'd finally turned off the lights, set the alarm, and headed out, Rocky and I were dragging but invigorated. "That was a good day, Boss," she said as we stopped outside the shop door.

"Boss? You don't need to call me boss, Rocky."

"I know I don't need, too, but I like to. Think of it like 'You da boss,' as in 'You're a badass.'"

I laughed. "So not as in *Who's the Boss?*"

Rocky's blank stare reminded me firmly of our age difference.

I waved a hand. "Never mind. Eighties reference."

She giggled. "I love that old-school stuff."

"Sure," I said as I tried not to roll my eyes. *Old school.* "Want to walk or drive over?"

"I'll drive," she said as I heard the beep of her car's alarm. "It'll save me the trouble later."

I waved as Mayhem and I started down the street. Spring was definitely here. It was still chilly, but the air felt damper, more green somehow. Plus, the lingering moments of dusk promised longer days. I was typically an autumn enthusiast, but this spring might just sway me to her favor.

Mayhem sniffed her way along the sidewalk, noting the earlier visitors and any gifts passersby had left in the way of crumbs. I enjoyed the window displays, particularly in the co-op. Cate had stopped by to suggest I take a look on my way home since they were featuring some of Woody's pieces. I'd mentioned wanting a small table to put behind my sofa, and she'd told me about a gorgeous one. It was indeed beautiful, but pricey – well-worth the price for such fine work, but I'd need a few more really good weekends to justify that kind of expense, even from a friend like Woody.

We were about to turn and head up our street when Mayhem stopped cold. Her hackles rose along her back, and the top of her head wrinkled. A low growl piled up in her throat.

I knelt down beside her. "You see something?" The growl got louder, and she turned to face behind me.

I spun around, but I didn't see anything. Mayhem didn't calm, though. In fact, she started to bark and tug hard at her leash. She was definitely seeing or hearing or smelling something.

Unsure what to do – I didn't want to turn my back on whoever or whatever might be back there, but I didn't want to go investigate either – I took a deep breath and decided our best course of action was to stay on the busier, if not really busy, Main Street. I held the leash tight and tugged Mayhem across the street, trying to act as if we were simply taking an evening stroll. If someone was following us, I didn't think they'd buy it, but maybe they'd have sense enough not to accost us in the full light of the street lamps.

We kept walking, picking up our pace a bit, the growl still climbing Mayhem's throat. I thought about heading back to the store and letting the alarm bring the police, but I didn't know how quickly I could fish out my keys. Plus, if it turned out to be nothing, I'd feel very foolish when the sheriff arrived.

I glanced in the shop windows as we practically jogged by. Everything looked fine, and I regretted my decision not to stop almost immediately when I heard footsteps behind me. I didn't dare look back lest I see someone lunging at me.

Quick as lightning, Mayhem lurched forward, dragging me into the street. I tried to slow her down, yelling *Stop* with my best "alpha dog" voice, but she kept going. She was either terrified, or . . .

Then, I saw where she was headed and heard the baying of a familiar hound dog voice. Daniel's shop was straight ahead, and the lights were on. We bolted into the garage, and Mayhem let out a volley of sharp barks.

Daniel came out of a door at a run, and I felt tears of relief spring to my eyes. "Harvey, are you okay?" He was by my side in seconds.

I fell into his chest and let out a hard sob. His arms came around my back and pulled me tight to him. A few moments later, when my sobs subsided, he pushed me gently away from him and asked, "You okay? What happened?"

I pointed toward a low stool at the side of the garage, and he walked me over so I could sit down. "I'm not sure, honestly. Mayhem heard or saw something, and she brought me here. I thought I heard footsteps behind us."

Daniel walked to the door and looked out with Mayhem at his heels. "I don't see anything, but I'm glad you came here."

"I didn't see anything either. But Mayhem doesn't usually act like that. Maybe she just smelled bacon." I tried to laugh.

"I doubt it. That's your girl. She knew you were in danger." His voice was serious.

"I feel silly. Maybe it was just my imagination. You guys were so worried. I guess I got a little spooked."

Daniel kneeled down to look into my face. "I don't know you well, Harvey, but you're not a person who scares easily, I can tell you that. If you – and Mayhem here – thought someone was out there, someone was out there."

I still felt a little ridiculous, but his confidence in my good sense was bolstering. To be believed is not a minor thing. I took a long, deep breath.

"Maybe you could walk me over for movie night?"

"I'd be honored, and if it's okay with you, I'll walk you home each night after this, too." He blushed a little. "I mean, until they catch the killer."

I winked at him. "But only until then. Once this murder is solved, I'm on my own."

"Right. Exactly." He put out his hand and helped me up. Then, he kept hold of my hand all the way to my house.

Movie night was perfect. Terrifying – especially after my scare earlier in the evening – but perfect. Somehow, being so scared that I had to keep my hand over my mouth because I kept making everyone else scream when I screamed took away some of the terror of earlier in the evening. But that didn't mean I wasn't scared.

Or that my friends were going to let me pretend I wasn't.

Mart had already cancelled an overnight trip for a consulting gig outside Philly, and Walter and Stephen had vowed to be at the store every minute for the next two days just as back-up. "Back-up for what?" I'd joked. "Will your organizational skills fend off an attacker?"

Stephen had thrown a pillow at me, and I'd smiled. Once again, I was reminded that I had good people around me.

After midnight, when *Us* ended, I walked Daniel to the door. I'd told him that he and Taco were welcome to crash on the couch, but he'd noted that Rocky seemed to have already claimed that honor. She had passed out halfway into the second movie, and when her phone had gone off, I'd answered her mom's text by telling her that Rocky was safe and could stay here for the night.

"Besides, Taco and I will sleep better in our own beds," Daniel said. Then he leaned in closer. "Do you need me to stay?"

"Oh no. I have plenty of company. It's just late, and well, I'd kind of like you to stay." I blushed at my candor. Adrenaline, hard cider, and fatigue made me brazen.

He gave me a tender smile. "I'd like to stay, too. But maybe our first sleepover can just be the two of us sometime."

I felt my heart kick hard against my chest. "I'd like that."

He leaned down and placed a tender kiss on my lips before turning and heading down the drive with Taco trailing behind at the speed of molasses.

His gentle kiss made sleep come easily, but in the middle of the night, I jerked awake and sent Aslan hissing to the floor. I'd had a nightmare about a giant paper flower chasing me down the street. That image haunted me until I got up, checked the doors, and made sure Mayhem was on the couch by the front door. She raised her head as I walked through. "Always on alert, aren't you, girl?" I gave her a good rub before heading back to try and sleep.

The next morning, I woke to the smell of bacon and came out to find all three of my closest friends dressed and cooking in the kitchen. "You guys are up and about early."

"Well, we have a bookstore to run," Walter said as he handed me my largest mug full of the darkest coffee I'd ever seen.

I smiled. "Thanks, guys. Really." The coffee was so good, and I was going to need it. I hadn't slept well after my nightmare, and if yesterday was an indication, it was going to be a doozy of a day at the shop.

After a quick shower, I took an extra second to slather on my favorite vanilla lotion before heading to the foyer to walk to the shop. As I passed Mart she said, "Ooh, vanilla. Someone's hopeful."

"What are you talking about?"

"Oh nothing," she said with a conspiratorial wink. "You just only wear vanilla when you feel really good about yourself."

I started to object, but then realized two things. My objection would do nothing but make me look defensive, and also, Mart was right. I did feel good about myself. A kiss from a handsome man will do that to a person.

All that good feeling faded away as we reached Main Street, though. One block up from the shop, the street was closed by a police car with its lights on, and I could see a group of people milling around on the sidewalks nearby. By some sort of tacit agreement, my friends and I crossed the street and passed by the commotion as far from it as possible. Maybe we knew that we'd just be in the way. Maybe we didn't want to be voyeurs about someone else's mishap. Or maybe we'd all just had enough adventure for the time being. But none of us tried to see what was going on.

Which was just as well because in a small town, nothing stays quiet for long. Within minutes, Woody had come in and found me. "You should know, Harvey. Deputy Williams was killed last night." I took a step back and ran into the wall of bookshelves behind me. "What?! Murdered. There on the street?"

"Well, not exactly on the street. She was in back of the stores here, by your parking lot."

I felt lightheaded. "Oh my word." I couldn't find anything else to say, so I just stood there and let the tears slide down my cheeks.

I hadn't known her well, but I did know her. And this was the second murder nearby in the past week. All that combined with my scare the night before had me near losing it in my own shop.

Just then, Daniel came in. He took one look at my face and grabbed a chair from the café. "Sit down, Harvey."

Walter stepped out from around the young adult bookshelf, studied my face, and headed to the back. Seconds later, he, Stephen, and Mart were there, all with looks of deep concern on their faces.

Woody told them what had happened, and Mart slid down the wall to sit on the floor. Walter and Stephen put their arms around one another. It was very quiet for a few moments.

Finally, I let out a shuddering breath and said, "Do they know what happened?"

"Apparently," Woody said, "she was doing her patrol about seven-thirty when someone ambushed her. Killed her instantly, it looks like."

"At least she didn't suffer," Stephen said as he glanced at me. I must have looked terrible because he said, "Harvey?!"

Mart looked up at Woody. "Did you say about seven-thirty?"

He nodded.

"It wasn't my imagination." I leaned my head back and stared at the ceiling. Mayhem had heard Deputy Williams' murder – that's what got her so scared – and I hadn't done a thing. "I could have helped her."

"Harvey Beckett, you need to stop it right now." Mart crawled over and put her face in mine. "You were almost a second victim."

"Third," I whispered.

"What?" Mart asked.

"I was almost the third victim."

Mart sighed. "Right. The third victim. If you had tried to help, you definitely would have been." She sank to the floor again and dropped her head into her hands. I thought she might be crying.

Daniel took my hand. "Mart's right, Harvey. Mayhem saved you."

Somewhere in the fog of shock, I could feel myself with two choices – give in and let myself fall apart or take a deep breath and move forward. I breathed in.

Then, I stood up. "I need to talk to the sheriff, tell him what happened to me last night. Maybe it will help."

Woody headed toward the door, "I'll get him."

"Is he okay?" I asked the older man as he opened the front door. "Were he and Deputy Williams close?"

"Not per se, I don't think. But then is anybody really okay when someone you know is killed?" He gave a sad smile and let the door close behind him.

Stephen looked me hard in the face and then asked, "What can I get you?"

I thought for a minute. "Chamomile tea with lots of honey and lemon." I needed to steady myself, slow down my heart rate.

"You got it," Stephen said and headed toward the café.

"You want to stay open?" Mart said.

"I do. Books help in a crisis. This is a way we can help. Let's put up a sign that says, 'Free coffee.' And I'll put together a display for the front table of books on grief and trauma."

Daniel put his arm around my shoulders. "Lead the way."

I steered us toward the psychology section to do what I could do – recommend books people needed.

Neighbors streamed into the store all day – some to have a cup of coffee, many to just see people from the community together. We didn't make a lot of sales, but it still felt like the shop was serving its purpose.

At one point, I came upon Marcus reading in the fiction section. He had a copy of Margaret Atwood's *Oryx and Crake* in his hand, and he was apparently so engrossed in the story that he didn't hear me walk up. "Oh, that book is amazing," I said, and he almost jumped to the ceiling.

He put a hand on his heart. "Shi—take mushrooms, Ms. Beckett. You scared me."

"I'm so sorry, Marcus." I sat down on the arm of the chair next to him. "You must really be liking this book."

"I am. You've read it?"

"Read the whole trilogy. Some of Atwood's best."

He smiled. "Yeah, I agree. I mean I loved *The Handmaid's Tale*, but this one, the science . . . I'm dying to read the next two."

This kid was a reader, an astute reader. I knew we'd been brought together for a reason. "Well, we have them when you're ready. You can sit right here and read the whole trilogy."

He looked down. "Really? I mean, I know these books are for sale."

"Really." I put my hand on his shoulder. "Any fan of Atwood can read here anytime. But mind if I ask a rude question – how did you hear about her? I mean, these books aren't—"

"Aren't exactly standard reading for a black man in America?" He was smiling, but I could also hear an edge in his voice. "My mom was an English teacher. She introduced me to *The Cat's Eye* back in eighth grade. Something about Atwood's stories just intrigues me. They're almost magical, but not quite . . . and there's always this thread of hope."

I patted his shoulder. "Exactly. I love her, too. When you're done with these, check out A. S. Byatt. Do you know her?"

"Only *Possession*, but if you recommend her other stuff, I'll totally read it."

This kid was amazing. "I'll put together a list." I smiled and stood up. "I'll let you get back to it."

That evening, we all sat around the shop floor – Mart, Stephen, Walter, Daniel, Woody, Rocky, and I – and passed cartons of Chinese food around. The store had been slammed. The news of the murder had traveled, so that brought more people to town than usual. Plus, the prominent mention on social media and the first of the real tourist trade had meant we were bustling as soon as the street was reopened.

The sheriff had come by late in the afternoon to get my statement about the night before. He'd looked haggard, worn down, raw. Rocky brought him a very large latte with extra, extra cream, and he drank it down in one gulp.

"Hard day, huh?"

"The hardest. Nothing about this job is particularly easy – except maybe the parades," he said with a weak smile. "But when it's someone you know . . ."

"Yeah." We sat in silence for a while.

"So someone was following you last night, Woody said?"

I shrugged. "I think so. I mean, I was really scared. And Mayhem was all kinds of worked up, but I didn't really see anything."

"Okay. Tell me exactly what happened."

After I reviewed the play-by-play of the night before, he said, "Yep, it sounds like Mayhem heard the murder. The timeline matches up almost perfectly. Too bad she can't testify."

I glanced over at my beautiful, red-headed pooch as she slept, again, butt to butt with Taco, and sent her a pulse of gratitude.

Then, an idea came to me. "Maybe she can. Do you have a minute?"

The sheriff gave me a puzzled look. "Sure. What do you have in mind?"

I called Mayhem over. "She definitely knew something was going on. Maybe she can sniff something out?"

The sheriff smiled. "I can see the headlines now, 'Local dog bests sheriff.'"

"I'm sure she'll give you all the credit."

I snapped on Mayhem's leash and told Daniel what was up. He leashed up Taco as official scent hound, and we headed out on the street while Mart watched the register.

"Too much activity out here on the street today, but maybe out back," I said as I led Mayhem around the building.

We let the dogs sniff and putter along the parking lot for a few minutes, and then, Taco started baying and was off. I had no idea a Basset Hound could move that fast, but Daniel was practically jogging to keep up. Then, Mayhem caught the scent, and I was sprinting along behind her. They were headed up the street toward Daniel's garage, which I could just see between buildings as we ran. Then, we darted off into the empty field behind the art co-op, and the dogs slowed to put their noses to the ground.

I'd seen hunters run dogs before, but I'd never been a big fan of chasing down an animal – either for sport or for the kill. So Mayhem had never been trained to hunt. But these dogs were hounds, and their scent instincts were kicking in hard. Within a minute, they'd centered in on a swatch of grass near the road, stopped, and stood stock still.

The sheriff gave me a look and headed over. There, glinting in the grass, was a knife with a long, thin blade. And at the tip, there was blood.

For the second time that day, a street in St. Marin's was closed off, and the entire police force of the county was on site. Fortunately for the store, most of the police activity was behind the building, so we'd stayed open and available for customers who just needed a place to rest or be distracted. But by the end of the day when the Chinese food had been delivered, courtesy of Rocky and her mom, we were all frazzled, exhausted, and full of questions.

"So this person really has something to hide? And Deputy Williams must have been on to it, you think?" Mart asked between mouthfuls of Lo Mein.

"Seems to be the case. Or at least the murderer thought she was on to it," Woody added.

I swallowed my bite of General Tso's chicken and said, "So we think it's the same person?"

"Pretty big coincidence if two murders happen in almost the same spot and aren't connected in some way?" Walter said.

"True." I put my chopsticks down and leaned back onto my elbows, knowing my back would regret this position in about two minutes. "Then, if that's the case, what did the deputy find?"

A silence settled in while everyone pondered what might have been worth killing for . . . twice.

"Do you think someone was trying to break in here again?" Daniel's voice sounded edgy, like he was angry, maybe. I was angry, though, so maybe I was reading more into what he was saying than was actually there.

"I think that's a possibility. I mean, you did say, Harvey, that Sheriff Mason had been really discreet about the umbrella. Maybe the murderer thinks it's still here."

I shuddered. "Glory, I hope not." I pondered installing a second alarm system.

Stephen reached over and patted my hand. "They moved the box inside. This time, when someone breaks in, we'll know."

"This time WHEN someone breaks in . . . " I could hear the panic in my own voice, but then laughed when I saw the smirk on my friend's face. "Stephen Murphy, you are the worst."

"Why thank you," he said with a little bow. "But seriously, a person would have to be pretty stupid to try to get in here again."

I knew he was right, but then, the murderer had stabbed a

deputy sheriff to death in the same place they'd killed Stevensmith. I started to giggle.

Daniel gave me a puzzled look. "Care to share with the class?"

"Well, I started thinking about one of my favorite shows of all time, *Buffy, The Vampire Slayer*, and how all these bad things happened at Sunnydale because there was a portal to hell there."

The entire group broke into laughter, and it felt like the weight of the day lifted a little. After a moment I said with fake seriousness, "So that's a no to the hell portal then?"

Stephen reached over and patted my knee. "That's a no. But if Willow shows, tell me. I love her."

"You got it."

We all walked back to our house together, and then quietly and without a hint of teasing, Mart, Stephen, and Walter went inside taking Mayhem with them. I turned to Daniel and found his face soft with worry. "You okay?"

I took a deep breath and gave myself a minute to really think about it. "I am. Dinner and a good laugh helped."

"I'm glad. Be careful, though, Harvey, okay?"

I nodded. "I will."

He gave me another soft kiss, and I slipped inside, not quite as elated as the night before.

I woke slowly on Sunday morning after a sleep so deep I wasn't sure I'd moved at all. My body ached in that delightful way it does after a good rest, and I stretched hard as I headed into the kitchen. My good mood immediately dropped when I saw my friends' faces. Mart was actually pale, which never happened given her love of a sunny day.

She gestured toward a bar stool and then spun the newspaper to face me. The headline read, "Local Bookshop Becomes Locus for Killing Spree." I gasped and then started to cry.

"It's not such a bad article, honey," Walter said as he came behind me to massage my shoulders. "Just a really atrocious headline."

"And it's just the *Courier*. Everyone here already knows about the murders." Mart's voice was breathless with desperate reassurance.

I wiped my eyes with a napkin and leaned back with the paper in front of me. Walter was right. The article wasn't that bad. In fact, they said a lot of good things about the store. The title wouldn't hurt the store, I knew. But the idea that a place I had created was associated with all this violent death really hurt.

Laying the paper on the counter, I stood and got a cup of coffee for myself. Then, I turned to my friends and said, "Time to get to work. We have a lot to do. Wear comfortable walking shoes." Then I turned and headed to my room, coffee mug in hand.

We all convened thirty minutes later in the foyer. My friends had no idea what I was thinking, but they'd all put on sneakers and were ready. I bent and put on Mayhem's brightest bowtie – she had one for each season and holiday thanks to Mart and her dog attire spree of 2017. Then, I looked at my friends and said, "It's time to give people a new association with our bookstore. No more 'Locus for a killing spree' for us."

"Alrighty then. What's the plan?" Stephen asked as he donned a bright red ball cap. "Handing out Rice Krispies treats? Hiring a pep band?" He gasped. "Giving away books?"

I smiled. "All good ideas, but no. We're going to solve this murder, but first, we're going to throw a party."

We needed to lift the mood in St. Marin's – I needed to lift the mood, and everyone loved a good street fair. So we spent the day planning for the first annual Leap Into Spring Street Fair for the following Sunday. A week wasn't much time to plan an event, but by the end of Sunday, we'd gotten most of the merchants on Main Street to agree to have a sale or giveaway table on the sidewalk in front of their shops, convinced the local restaurants to offer a special spring dish on their menus, secured commitments from three of Baltimore's favorite food trucks to come out for the day, and sent press releases to all the local media. We were billing the day as a "Celebration for the Life of Deputy Skye Williams."

When the shop closed after a mediocre sales day – only the true crime enthusiasts seemed excited by shopping at "murder central," as one customer put it – I was still feeling pretty good about the plan for the following weekend. But I was also more determined than ever to solve this murder. I wanted the sheriff to be able to announce he'd made an arrest at the festival. Of course, I hadn't told anyone that – it seemed a ridiculous goal, but still, when I put my mind to something, I was hard to stop.

After we closed up, I sent Mart, Stephen, and Walter home after assuring them that Daniel would be there in a few minutes to walk me home. I had to show them his text message saying just that and lock the door while they watched before they would leave. But finally, I had a few minutes to myself. I loved my friends, but I was worn down by constant people. My little introvert heart needed just a few moments alone.

Plus, I wanted to take a look behind the shop right quick because something had been bugging me since the day before, and I needed to see the parking lot now that it was almost dark. I could almost hear Daniel scold me as I pushed open the back door, but I had Mayhem on her leash and a hammer in my hand.

I walked out into the lot a ways after taking a good look to be sure I was alone. I could see clear to the tree line that ran beside the houses on the block over, and all the way down the street, the lights on the back of the shops showed an empty back alley. No one in sight.

Turning to face the building, I studied the back of my store. It looked like the back of a gas station, except that the doorways for what used to be the outdoor bathrooms – one for men and one for women – were closed off from the inside. They would have opened into the bathrooms inside if they worked, but I didn't love the idea of customers having to go around the building to, well, "go." So I'd had the contractors move the doors inside and close these off. But when we'd been back here looking for the knife, I'd noticed that the left-hand door looked dingy and had made a mental note to paint it again.

The fact that one door had gotten dirty and the other hadn't bugged me, though, and I wanted to see if there was a problem with the gutter or something. I got closer, and that's when I noticed the smell. *Oregano?* No, sage. I knew that smell from almost every shop in the Haight in San Francisco. It was the scent du jour of the wellness community, but I had never cared for it much since it was so deeply appropriative to take a Native American ritual and use it to make a store smell good.

I got closer and saw a pile of ash on the ground by the door. Someone had been burning sage? Presumably they thought the place had bad energy and had been smudging the doorway, but who? And why? And for how long? Something had been burned here a lot to turn that door a slightly gray hue.

I was almost certain that I was smelling sage, but I couldn't be sure. *I need to get a sample and have it analyzed,* I thought and then immediately wondered if that was even a thing investigators did or just a result of my deep affection for TV police procedurals. *Better safe than sorry.* I dug into my back pocket and pulled out a candy wrapper that I'd shoved there earlier. I was always putting trash in my pockets – a gum wrapper someone had dropped in the store, a bottle top on the sidewalk – and it drove Mart crazy when she did laundry. "Ooh, you don't know where that's been, and you put it in your clothing." I always shrugged. Now, I had good reason for my trash.

I took a quick look around to be sure I was still alone and then set down the hammer. Then, I used the tip of my pinky finger to scoot a little of the ash into the wrapper and twisted it shut before carefully sliding the filled wrapper into my front pocket. I scooped up the hammer and made my way over to the back door. I slammed it shut, dropped the safety bar into place, and stood stock-still, listening to be sure no one was on the other side of the door. I didn't hear anything, so I let out a long sigh and headed toward the front of the store.

Mayhem, however, didn't follow. She stood staring at the back door until a knock at the window signaled Daniel and Taco's arrival. Only then, did she join me by the alarm box and then lead me out the front door. I appreciated her vigilance, but I hoped it was just over-caution and not a response to someone outside.

As we headed down Main Street, I told Daniel about the back door and the ash I'd found. I wanted to be annoyed that he was more concerned about me being behind the shop alone than he was curious about the ash, but I couldn't be. It just made me want to smile to see his concern, but I figured grinning away as he expressed that feeling probably wasn't the best idea.

We decided we should probably let the sheriff know about the door right away, just in case, so after I texted Mart to let her know we'd be a bit late *and* answered her call when she confirmed I wasn't texting under duress *and* let her hear Daniel's voice to triple check, we walked over to Mason's office. I didn't know if he'd be there, but I figured I could leave a note and the wrapper – preferably transferred to something a little more secure – with the officer on duty.

But we didn't even need the note. The sheriff was the officer on duty for the night, a fact that made me like him more. I always respected a person who did all the things they required the people who worked for them to do.

After I explained about the door and endured a less pleasant lecture not only about the risk I had taken to gather the evidence but also about how there were trained police officers in town that had phones, Mason took the wrapper, poured the contents into an evidence bag, and then said, "This makes things more interesting."

"It does?" I sat forward on the edge of the hard, plastic chair next to his desk. "Why?"

"Slow down, Cowgirl," Mason said. "Did you not hear me about trained investigators?"

I sat back and rested my hands on my knees. "I did, but can I help it if I'm a naturally curious person?"

Daniel and the sheriff exchanged a look that said, "So that's what she calls it," before the sheriff turned to me. "I expect if I don't tell you, you'll be back at the library looking through microfilm again. Oh, you thought I didn't know about that, huh?"

I cleared my throat. "I guess there are no secrets in this town."

"Not when the new woman is poking her nose into a murder

investigation. Nope, no secrets then." He gave me a stern look down his nose. "Anyway, we found a similar pile of ash over at the courthouse."

"In the courthouse?" Daniel asked.

"Well, not in there, but by the old 'colored' bathrooms outside." The corners of his mouth turned down hard when he said *colored*.

"Oh man. I grew up in the South, but I'll never get used to the fact that black people had to use separate facilities." I looked at the sheriff. "I'm so sorry. Is that hard for you to think about?" I felt naïve asking that question, but to talk about segregation with a black man and not at least acknowledge that this history was his parents' reality felt ridiculous, not to mention racist.

"It used to be. Still is if I think about it too much. But it was the way it was, so I just work with that." He looked at me then. "Thanks for asking."

"No problem. But this was found at the colored restrooms? The men's room?"

"Yep, same as at your place."

I tilted my head. "Really? Were the bathrooms at the gas station for black people?"

He sat back then. "Oh, you didn't know? Oh yeah, that station was owned by a black family, the Hudsons. It was even in *The Green Book*."

I knew *The Green Book* – that little booklet that told African American people where they could safely sleep, eat, and shop as they traveled through the segregated South. They'd made that movie with Mahershala Ali and Viggo Mortenson and used the book's name as the title. A lot of people loved that film; It even won the Oscar, but when I'd seen it at a theater in Oakland, the conversation in the lobby afterward wasn't so flattering. One woman said, "Just what we needed, another movie about white people saving us." I'd liked the movie, but what that woman said stuck with me.

But it wasn't the film that Mason was talking about – it was the actual book, and I was surprised. "It was? Wow." I sat quietly for a moment, pondering the history of my little shop's building.

Mason furrowed his brow. "Does that bother you?"

"What?! Oh, no. I love that actually. I like that it was a safe space for people. I'm just thinking about what it must have been like to need to consult a book to be able to know you were safe. I mean, I get the idea of safe spaces because as a woman I think about that stuff. I don't go into a parking garage alone at night, for example—"

"But you will go into a dark parking lot where two murders have happened alone." Daniel's tone was playful, but he had a point.

I gave him a gentle smile. "You're right. But I guess I'm saying I understand the experience of feeling unsafe sometimes, but never to that level. Never so much that I had to know which towns I could drive in at night and which were Sundown Towns, where I'd be in danger if I was there after dark." In one of the local history books I'd read when I first moved to St. Marin's, I'd read about an island a bit further down the shore, where black people couldn't visit after dark for fear of their lives. The book had called it a Sundown Town, and I'd learned about another facet of racism I'd never been taught.

"Well, I'm glad you like knowing that history, Harvey, but it does beg the question, why be burning sage at the door to two bathrooms that historically only black men used?"

I nodded. That was a good question, and I was eager to try and find out.

We left the sheriff's office and had to wake up Mayhem and Taco where they snoozed by the bike rack out front. As we walked home, I ran through my thoughts out loud. I had always been a verbal processor, and so things really only became clear to me when I talked through them. It was a habit both of my parents, who believed firmly that personal problems needed to remain so private that they weren't even shared with family, despised. Mom would pick me up after school and ask how my day was, but when I began to tell her about the girl on the playground who had told me to "mind my own beeswax" when I'd asked what she was doing or some such thing, Mom would say, "Now, dear, we don't need to relive all the hard moments do we? What would you like for dinner?" And just like that, the conversation would be over.

Daniel, however, didn't seem to mind at all. In fact, he was listening intently enough that when I started talking about how awful it must have been to have to wait for a bathroom that might be hundreds of miles off, he told me a story about an older man from St. Marin's whose parents had once had to drive the entire length of the Eastern Shore, from Cape Charles, Virginia, to St. Marin's – a distance of over 150 miles – with him as a toddler who had to go to the bathroom because they'd forgotten their *Green Book* and didn't know where it was safe to stop.

I shook my head. "People can be absolutely horrible."

Daniel nodded. "Yes. Yes, we can."

Chapter Eight

The next morning, almost as soon as I got the shop open, the phone started ringing. I cringed every time, thinking it was going to be some reporter who wanted to write a story on "murder central." But each time, it was someone inquiring about the street fair and often asking if there was a fund set up for Deputy Williams' family.

I was glad that the sheriff's office had established a scholarship fund in her honor. She wasn't married and didn't have children, and the town was covering her funeral expenses, so this was a great way to honor her memory and give her a new legacy in the community. One local high schooler who wanted to go into law enforcement would receive a scholarship for training each year. By the sound of the callers, that fund was going to be set for a long time to come.

Walter and Stephen came by on their way to BWI for their flight just before noon, and I gave them both huge hugs. "Thank you so much for coming. I wish you could stay longer, see how the street fair goes."

"Us, too, but work calls," Stephen said with a frown. "I'm so glad we got to see you in *your shop*, my friend. Now, be safe, okay?"

Walter put an arm around my shoulders. "No sleuthing without help."

I wrapped my arms around his waist and squeezed. "Agreed."

As I walked them to the door, I said, "Text me when you land, okay?"

"You sure about that?" Stephen asked. "It'll be late."

"I'm sure." I'd always wanted my parents to ask that of me, so I tried to ask it of friends when they travelled.

I watched them load their bags into the waiting Uber and brushed away a tear. Rocky sidled up to me and slid a hot cup of Earl Grey into my hands. The warm smell of bergamot soothed me, and when I took a sip, it was hot – but not scalding – with lots of milk and sugar, just as I liked it. "Thank you," I whispered as I leaned my head on her shoulder.

We stood quietly like that, looking out at the overcast day. It was a perfect reading day, and I hoped that would mean we'd have some customers. But in the meantime, I had work to do. I gave Rocky a kiss on the cheek and said thank you before heading to the counter to figure out what exactly I could have on hand for the weekend's activities.

Throughout the afternoon, the flow of customers was quiet but steady, with lots of folks picking up stacks of books and magazines and enjoying the café tables. Some booksellers hated that practice because it meant books got stained and grungy and that there'd be a lot of clean-up. But personally, I loved it. While I needed to make money, for sure, I also just loved when people read, and if that meant they camped out at a table for two hours with *Garden and Gun* and a copy of *Into Great Silence*, I was fine with that. Plus, they almost always bought something, and the most conscientious folks purchased anything they got a crumb on. I appreciated the courtesy even if I didn't require it.

While they read, I decided to order a bunch of children's books – some picture books, some board books, some easy readers, some chapter books – and then do a "mystery book buy" for the street festival. I'd wrap the books in brown paper and let the kids pick any book they wanted from a bin for their age group. All books would be two dollars, but you had to keep what you got or find another kid to swap with. I figured this would cover my costs but give some families who might not be able to get books a chance to pick some up . . . and maybe it'd even be a social thing for the kids, too, like a less heartless version of that holiday gift exchange where you get to steal the gift you want most.

Mart checked in about a billion times throughout the day, and even Stephen dropped a text from the airport to remind me to *use the buddy system when sleuthing.* My friends cared . . . and they were annoying.

I knew Daniel was planning on meeting me at the shop at closing, so when the bell chimed as I was counting out the register, I expected to look up and see him. Instead, Max Davies was there. He had the studied stance of someone trying to look casual, one foot out to the side, a book in his hands. But he kept cutting his eyes over to me, and as soon as I got to a stopping place, I closed the register drawer and said, "Well, hello, Max. Nice to see you."

"Oh, hi, Harvey," he said, "I didn't see you there."

I wanted to roll my eyes, but I restrained myself. "Well, here I am. What can I do for you?"

He put down the book – a copy of Michelle Obama's *Becoming* – and walked over. "Since you asked . . . I was wondering if you could help me with something for the street festival."

I was surprised. Max hadn't replied to my query of merchants on Main Street, so I figured he had chosen not to participate. This visit had just gotten much more positive than his last one. "Sure, what can I do?"

"You can call it off."

I stepped back a bit. "What?! Why?" My hopes for a good conversation were dashed. I was back to finding the man annoying.

"Because there's a murderer on the loose, and you're asking everyone to stand around out in the middle of all those people. We'll be sitting ducks."

I didn't take the opportunity to note that he had just walked into my store on a quiet Monday night when almost no one was around and that if the killer wanted to get him, they'd probably do so as he left. It didn't feel kind to point out the obvious.

I pointed toward the café and trailed behind Max just slowly enough to text Daniel, tell him to come on in but be discreet. *Max is here to talk me out of the fair.*

Daniel's response was perfect. *Oh glory!*

Max took a seat by the window – another perfect opportunity for the murderer to take him out, I thought – and proceeded to tell me how it just wasn't prudent to draw us all out in the open like that. "It'll be the perfect opportunity."

I had to stifle a giggle when I remembered how a group of my college friends had come home to Chesapeake City with me and been terrified that an ax murderer would find us out on the secluded road to my family home. "There are no street lights," my friend from Long Island had said. I had tried to point out that the chances of a murderer being around were far greater in a crowd, but their fear – like all fear – wasn't based in logic. So they spent the weekend with every light in the house on so they'd see the ax murderer when he came for them.

Now Max had the opposite fear – that the murderer would find it easier to kill someone in a crowd. I let out a long slow breath to steady my thoughts. "I see your point. But what makes you think the murderer will strike again?"

"These things always happen in threes," he said without any sense of irony or shame. "We've had two murders. We're just waiting for the third."

I heard the bell tinkle and saw Daniel and Taco come in quietly and take a seat in the chair-and-a-half by the fiction section, close enough to hear but not close enough to intrude.

"Ah, I have heard that theory about tragedy," I said, drawing my attention back to Max. "But if that's the case, wouldn't the murderer want to act more quickly, get it over with rather than waiting another week?"

He did not show me the courtesy of trying to restrain his eye roll. "Serial killers work on a schedule, Harvey." He gave an exaggerated glance around the shop. "For someone who runs a bookshop, you aren't very well informed."

I swallowed hard, gave Daniel a discreet raised eyebrow over

Max's shoulder, and said, "I hadn't realized the person who killed Ms. Stevensmith and Ms. Williams was a serial killer."

He let out a long sigh. "Clearly, the killer has a type. Two women. Both in their forties. Both in public roles." He paused and looked at the wall above and behind my head. "But now that I say that, I realize I need not worry. I'm not the killer's type." He stood up. "I'm sorry to have taken your time, Harvey. Carry on with the street fair."

He spun on a heel and headed toward the front door without giving Daniel even a nod.

As soon as the bell rang, Daniel guffawed with such exuberance that I thought his belly must hurt from holding that in. "Someone's been watching too much *Criminal Minds*," he said as soon as he stopped laughing.

I grinned. "Clearly, I need to spend more time in my True Crime section lest my ignorance of serial killer practices lead me astray into planning more fundraisers in my folly."

Still laughing, I gave Daniel's arm a squeeze as I passed by him to grab my coat and set the alarm. Then, we headed out into the cool air of a spring evening.

I spent the next morning arranging the new books on the front table. New release day was quickly becoming my favorite day of the week. I loved all those new covers, and the smell – all fresh wood and ink. It always took me back to the construction sites in my child-hood neighborhood. Ours was one of the first houses built, but soon, new homes were going up everywhere. I spent many an after-noon climbing around on second floors that just had the studs up for walls and savoring the smell of all that fresh timber.

Cate and Henri, the weaver from the co-op, came by mid-day and brought the most amazing curry soup – sweet potatoes, coconut milk, and just enough heat to make my nose tingle. I ate three bowls. We sat on stools behind the register and gobbled down the goodness. Henri had just started a catering business, and she had asked Cate to help her find people to sample her wares. I told the stellar cook that if everything was this good, I'd sample anything . . . and use her to cater bookstore events once I had more cash flow.

"I'd love that," Henri said. "Plus, I know Rocky and her mom Phoebe from church. Maybe we could coordinate together – they do the sweets, I do the savories."

"I'm getting hungry all over again at just the thought."

"Alright, back to work with me. Thanks for being a taste tester, Harvey."

"Thank *you*. Come by anytime, especially if you bring snacks." Henri waved as she headed out.

Cate helped me clean up the lunch trash and said, "I have to admit, I had another motive for stopping by."

"You're looking for the friends and family bookstore discount?" I looked at her out of the corner of my eye as we tucked our stools back against the counter.

"Well, no, but let's come back to that," she chuckled. "Actually, it's about the murders."

"Ah," I said. "Most things are these days. What's up?"

"Well, I was in Elle Heron's stand the other day to pick up some roses Lucas needed for a museum event. Elle had gone into the back to get the flowers, and I was just standing around by the counter. I happened to notice a stack of newspapers, so I picked up the top one. It was from a few years ago, which I thought was odd. Who keeps old newspapers?"

I nodded. I knew a few people, but their houses kind of looked like those mazes they force mice to run through in laboratories.

"I got curious, so I rifled through the rest of the papers. All of them were old, some of them from a decade ago. I couldn't stop myself, and I flipped through a few of the papers. You won't believe what I found?"

"A baby otter? No, wait, the secret for turning lead into gold? No, wait, this has to be it – articles?"

Cate snickered. "Alright, smarty pants. Yes, articles. But the interesting part was which ones were highlighted."

Ah, now I was interested. "Which ones?"

"Every article by Lucia Stevensmith."

"Every article? That's a lot of articles. The woman was verbose to say the least."

"Yep, pretty much an article on every page had one or more headings highlighted in yellow." Cate sounded pleased with herself, and I couldn't blame her. This was very intriguing.

"Anything else you noticed?"

"Nope, Elle came back, and I didn't want to get caught." She paused. "I don't really know why. It just felt like she might be embarrassed for someone to be snooping through her papers."

I nodded. "Right, especially when you've marked every article a murdered woman ever wrote."

"I know, right? That's why it seemed a little suspicious to me."

I wasn't sure *suspicious* is the word I'd use, but it was definitely odd and worth further exploration. "Thanks, Cate. I appreciate you telling me."

"Think I should tell the sheriff?"

"That you found some old newspapers with articles highlighted? Nah. I'll look into it."

"Harvey." Her voice was low and foreboding. "What about being careful? Stephen and Walter made me promise."

I tried to give my most innocent look by batting my eyelashes. "I'm not doing anything dangerous, just going to talk to another storeowner."

Cate squinted at me. "Sure. Sure." She picked up her purse. "Want to go now? I actually need to get more baby's breath, so it's a great excuse."

I took a look around the store. A couple of browsers, but nothing Rocky couldn't handle. I ran over to the café and checked to be sure she was okay to manage things for a bit, got her okay, and rushed back. "I have thirty minutes."

"Let's not dawdle then."

Elle's stand smelled like chrysanthemums. It was a smell I loved, even though I resented the flowers themselves a bit. In high school, secret admirers always gave out mums on Valentine's Day. I'd never gotten a single flower. It was easier to blame the bloom than the people.

"You're back," Elle said as she came out from the cooler. "Forget something?"

Cate stepped to the counter. "Actually yes. I need more baby's breath. Right now, we look like we're throwing a proposal party in the museum conference room. I need to lighten the intensity a bit."

"Well, then I don't know if baby's breath is the way to go. Too much like a boutonniere." Elle put her hands behind her head and looked up at the ceiling. "What if you did small daisies instead? I just got a big bunch in, and they're not only pretty but they're cheap."

"Perfect," Cate said. "Harvey, do you want something for the store?" She kicked me in the shin as she spoke.

"Um, what? Oh yeah, for the street fair actually. I mean, I don't want to get into your sales territory or anything, but I did think I'd put some small vases around the shop and café for Sunday. Have anything that would work?"

"Hmmm. You're thinking about using those antique bottles you used for the grand opening, right?"

"Good memory," I said. I'd collected old bottles from junk stores for weeks and then used them as vases for the shop. Unique and cheap. "Yeah, so something that looks good with a short stem."

"I suppose dandelions won't work," she said with a grin.

"I'm not opposed, but I'd rather not have everyone blowing seeds around the shop on day three. Way too much sweeping for me."

"Fair enough." She tapped a finger against the clear frame of her glasses. "What about hyacinths? Totally seasonal, very hardy, perfect size."

"I love it. Maybe forty to fifty stems?"

"You got it. I'll bring them over Saturday if that suits."

She started to head back to get Cate's daisies, but before she went, I said, "So these murders, huh?" I felt like a bonehead – how obvious could I be? – but it was the best I could do on the spur of the moment.

Cate wandered off to look at the arrangements in the cooler, presumably to take away a bit of the pressure and make it seem less like I was interrogating Elle. I was grateful.

"Gracious. Just awful." She pressed both hands down on the counter. "I know that everyone says this, but I can't believe someone was murdered in our town."

I nodded. I couldn't believe it either. Somehow it had been easier to take in a murder in San Francisco. Not easy, of course, but easier. I guess I expected it more there. "Tell me about it."

Her head jutted up. "Oh, and it happened in your shop. Here I am thinking about the reputation of our town, and you had a murder happen in your new store. How awful!" She came around the counter then. "How are you?"

I felt tears threaten, but I didn't think I'd get much information if I was crying. "It's been a hard couple of weeks, to be honest. But the shop is doing well in spite of everything."

She gave my arm a squeeze. "Maybe in part because of everything." She winced. "Is that an awful thing to say?"

I laughed softly. "No, it's not awful. It's the truth. The 'no press is bad press' rule certainly applies here."

The counter was filled with buckets of daylilies, and I ran my fingers lightly over the petals. "What's got me puzzled," I said, "is why Stevensmith? I mean she wasn't very likable, but what had she done to make someone mad enough to murder her?"

Elle's face went blank, and she looked down at the floor before quickly collecting herself and giving an exaggerated shrug. "That's a good question. I expect whoever did it felt like they had a good reason – either that or it was a crime of passion. I mean, she made a lot of people angry, including our neighbor Max. Either way," she said as she stepped back behind the counter, "I'm sure the sheriff will sort it all out. I'm just sad the murderer wasn't caught before Skye was killed. That was such a tragedy."

She let out a hard sigh and went into the back room.

"The deputy's murder was a tragedy, but not Stevensmith's?" Cate asked as she slid back over beside me.

"She didn't say that." I felt like I needed to defend Elle for some reason, but even I had to admit that she wasn't exactly giving off the "completely innocent" vibe.

"She didn't have to say it." Cate gave me a look that said, if it quacks like a duck.

Eleanor came back from the storeroom with an armload of small-petaled daisies. They were beautiful and seemed like the perfect emblem of spring. They would definitely lower the intensity of Cate's roses.

Cate paid, and we thanked Elle and made plans for her to come by on Saturday afternoon to drop off the flowers. Except for that whole suspicion of murder thing, it would have been a lovely visit with a neighbor.

***

Back at the shop, things had gotten much busier in the twenty-five minutes we'd been gone, and I could see the look of relief on Rocky's face when we came in. She had a line at the café counter and was just ringing up a big sale at the book register. "I've got this," I said as I slid in beside her.

"Thank you. The need for caffeine was getting palpable," she whispered as she jogged out from behind the counter toward the café.

I laughed and continued ringing up the man in front of me. His selections were fascinating. Most men stick to the supposedly "male" genres like thrillers and spy fiction, military history, maybe a bit of literary fiction as long as the main characters are men. But this guy was buying a stack of cozy mysteries by some of my favorites: Mollie Cox Bryan, Maggie Sefton, and Millie Jordan. "Lots of murder here," I said with an ironic wink.

Well, just when I needed to restock my supply for the week, I thought. "What better place to come than the bookstore that was the scene of the crime?" He gave me a tentative smile. "I hope that doesn't bother you."

"Not at all." I was surprised I meant that when I said it. "We're just glad people are finding us. I love a lot of these books, but I hope you don't mind me saying that I don't find many men who read cozy mysteries."

He shrugged. "Yeah, I know. I'm an anomaly, but since my wife died, I just want to read books that capture my attention, let me feel like I'm among friends, and give me a chuckle at the sleuth's complete inability to walk away."

I felt color run up my neck. He'd pegged me pretty well. I managed to choke back my embarrassment and say, "Well, if you ever need recommendations—"

"Oh, I'll be back. I went with some favorite authors here, but I saw a couple of writers I don't know yet. Maybe you can point me toward some great books when I come next time."

"I'd love that. I'm Harvey, by the way. I own the shop."

"Galen Gilbert. Nice to meet you. I have decided that I'll make St. Marin's my Tuesday outing – I have one for each day of the week just so that I don't get to be too much of a homebody – so I'll see you in a week."

I watched the small, gray-haired, white man as he made his way out the front door. A customer like that was why I was in business. I knew books could save people's lives – keep them from deep heartbreak like the loss of a partner – and I immediately started musing on what cozy mysteries to recommend next. Maybe something British?

That night, I went home exhausted. Daniel and Taco walked Mayhem and me home as usual, but when we got to the door, I put my hand on his chest when he leaned down to give me his single kiss. "Let's hold that thought," I smiled at the shock and then the sadness in his eyes. "Want to come in, eat a huge bowl of peanut butter popcorn, and then complain about our aching bellies while we binge watch *Game of Thrones*? I've never seen it, and I hear it's best if I not go in alone." The events of the past ten days had finally caught up with me, and Mart was away. I didn't feel like doing anything strenuous like cooking a meal, but I did feel like spending more time with Daniel.

He took my keys and unlocked the door. "After you, Madame."

Peanut butter popcorn is one of those foods that the world needs to know about. It's a really simple thing to make – just honey (or corn syrup if you must), sugar, peanut butter, and vanilla all mixed together and poured over popcorn. The only problem with this is that it is possible – but not advisable – to eat an entire bowl by oneself. This was my other motivation for inviting Daniel in. I'd been thinking about this popcorn all day, and if he shared, at least I wouldn't make myself too sick.

I mixed the peanut butter sauce while he used the air popper to make the popcorn and fed Taco and Mayhem. They would have been content with popcorn for dinner, too, but we opted for kibble instead. Then, he watched as I dumped the popcorn into a super-big metal bowl and then poured the peanut butter sauce over top, stirring carefully enough to get sauce on most of the kernels but not so carefully that we'd miss out on the goodness of extra sauce at the bottom of the bowl. "That's the best part," I told him as I explained my strategy.

We sat cross-legged on the sofa, our knees touching and the bowl of popcorn wedged between us, and I felt myself completely relax for the first time in weeks. Daniel loved the popcorn, and the twenty minutes of *Game of Thrones* that I saw before I fell asleep looked pretty intriguing.

When I woke up the next morning, I was under my favorite quilt – the one that usually graced my bed, Mayhem and Taco were on the floor beside me, and Daniel had left a note on the coffee table. "Dear Harvey, I didn't want to wake you. You needed the rest, but I did take the popcorn. I will return the bowl when I bring your keys to the shop at 9:30. I left Taco behind because he and Mayhem make a good guard duty pair, and also, I didn't want to carry him home. See you soon. xo"

I sat up and stretched and smiled. This guy, this one was a keeper.

Chapter Nine

Daniel hadn't stayed long when he'd dropped off the completely empty and washed popcorn bowl and my keys, but it was still nice to start the day seeing him. I wasn't sure what to make of the fact that he watched three episodes of *Game of Thrones* without me and now had to – by my demand – wait for me to catch up with him, but I figured I'd forgive him, by oh, say, noon.

I spent the first part of my morning swapping the display of Westerns I had made with a new display of True Crime books, featuring my favorite title, *Shot in the Heart* by Mikal Gilmore. I knew we had a number of loyal readers for Westerns, but I needed to be wise and go with what All Booked Up was known for, and right now, that was crime. So True Crime got the coveted face-out shelves just behind the new release tables. I knew where my bread was buttered.

I was just about to head out to the taco truck and get Rocky and me some lunch when Divina Stevensmith came through the front door. After our last conversation and her odd reaction to the color orange, I felt the impulse to run around and tug all the books with orange covers off the shelves, but I resisted. After all, she just said she didn't like the color; she didn't say it made her homicidal or anything.

The tiny woman was wearing a polka dot jumpsuit that reminded me of the rain coat she'd been wearing that first time I saw her, and I wondered if she had a penchant for the whimsical print. I was on my way to ask her that very question as a casual conversation starter when she made an abrupt turn away from the self-help section that she'd been browsing and walked straight toward me.

I mentally braced myself for what looked like it might be a dressing down, given her forceful march in my direction, but when she reached me, she said, "Thank you for what you're doing for Deputy Williams and the town." Her voice was quiet and steady. "That poor woman. She didn't deserve that."

Ms. Stevensmith was twisting a bright blue scarf in her hands, and she looked on the verge of tears. I came around the counter and pointed to a pair of club chairs by the art books. "Want to sit?"

She gave a small nod and lowered herself smoothly into the nearest chair. Next to her, I looked a bit like a cow trying to use furniture, but I tried to focus on her nervousness.

"It was a sad thing, her death, especially for you."

She nodded, scarf still twisting. "And I'm sorry you have been affected, and in your new shop and all. What terrible timing."

I looked around the shop. "Well, if it hadn't happened here, it probably would have happened somewhere."

Her eyes darted to meet mine. "I don't know about that. I mean, there's something about this space, don't you think?" She stood up and spun in a circle as if trying to see the whole shop. "There's a lot of history here."

I thought about what the sheriff had told me about *The Green Book* and this building when it was a gas station. Ms. Stevensmith was easily in her eighties, very much someone who had grown up in the Jim Crow South. "You knew this building when it was a gas station?"

"Knew it? Harvey, my husband owned it."

I dropped my chin to look at her through the tops of my eyes. "I'm confused. I thought the man who owned the gas station was black."

She grinned. "He was." She took a deep breath and looked at me closely.

"Okay, but, forgive me for asking, but wasn't Lucia white? Not biracial, I mean?" Conversations around race were always so hard.

"Yes, you're right, not that everyone who has mixed-race ancestry shows it the way we think they would, of course."

I nodded, although that was news to me.

"Lucia was my daughter from my second marriage. Her father was white. My first husband, Berkeley Hudson, owned the gas station." She sat down and looked at me. "He was black."

"I heard that the station was in *The Green Book*."

"It was . . . although a few places in there were owned by white people, too. But most were black-owned. Berkeley's was one of them." She smiled and seemed to slide back into her memories. "Lots of people came through here when they were on their way from New York or Philly and headed to Norfolk or other places in the South. No I-95 then, you know?"

I hadn't known, but I loved trivia like that. "Anyone famous?"

"Oh my, yes. John Lee Hooker stopped once, ended up having dinner with us because there wasn't anywhere else to eat until you got to Norfolk. I couldn't get him to play for us, but he was mighty nice."

"You met John Lee Hooker?" I was tempted to get up and put his music over the speakers right now.

She gave me a soft grin. "I did. My favorite guest, though, Richard Wright—"

I couldn't help myself and interrupted her. "Richard Wright stopped in St. Marin's. What?!"

"A fan are you?"

"You could say that. I've read *Native Son* maybe twenty times. He's one of the best American writers in history."

"And a big fan of meatloaf," she said with a smirk, "With extra ketchup."

"No?! Really? I love that."

She got quiet then and folded her hands around her scarf. "It was an important place, this gas station. A haven for a lot of folks who just needed somewhere to stop and rest before heading on."

I put a hand on her knee. "It was kind of you to open your home."

"Maybe too kind." She stood up and looked toward the back of the store. "Anyway," she said with a little shake of her head, "I'm glad you own this place, Ms. Beckett. It seems like you appreciate the stories – both the ones in the air and the ones on the page – that live in these walls."

I felt like I was not getting the whole picture here, but she was clearly moving our conversation along, so I didn't push. "Thank you, Ms. Stevensmith. I really appreciate that." I took a few steps back toward the counter. "Was there something I could help you with? Something you needed."

"Oh yes, I almost forgot. I'd like to donate a piece to auction off at the street fair with all proceeds going to the scholarship fund in honor of Deputy Williams, if that might be alright with you."

"Alright with me? Of course. That's lovely. Can you get me a bit of information about the piece, and I'll get the word out to the press? I'm sure this will bring some folks out."

She handed me a small sheet of paper covered in neat handwriting. "I took the liberty of anticipating that request and made some notes here. Just let me know if you need anything further."

I glanced down at the paper and saw she'd written:

Divina Stevensmith – 1938-
Study of St. Marin's at Nightfall
Paper Collage
8' x 12.5'
Valued at $25,000

"Oh my word, Ms. Stevensmith. This is too generous. I had no idea—"

"No idea my work was worth that much?" She smiled demurely. "I hope I'm not overvaluing my art, but I sold a piece that size last week for a little more than that. So I hope that's fair, but feel free to lower the value if you think it appropriate. You're welcome to come by and see the piece in my studio if that would help. And of course, people don't need to bid nearly that much—"

"No, of course your work is worth that much and more. I'm just stunned by your generosity. Thank you." I took a deep breath and then leaned down to give the tiny woman a hug. "Truly. Thank you. This is a huge gift in Deputy Williams' honor."

"It's the least I could do." She gave my hand a hard squeeze.

As she started to walk toward the door, I called after her, "Ms. Stevensmith, can I ask a question?"

She turned, and I met her near the doorway. "I mean, I'm just curious. The color orange? You really seemed to dislike it. Is that an artistic thing? Something about the way it, um, plays with other colors or such?"

That tiny woman looked me dead in the eye and laughed so hard her shoulders shook. "Oh my, no. I've just seen way too much of it in my day. Lucia loved orange from the time she was a little girl. She wanted her room painted orange, always wore orange clothes, even now – er, until she died – she took notes on orange paper. I just got tired of it, you know, the way you get tired of a food if you eat it all the time, even if you loved it once."

"Ah, thank you. I totally get it. Sometime, I'll tell you about my small overaffection-turned-distaste for Reese's peanut butter cups. Thanks for telling me. I had been curious."

She placed her hand on my shoulder. "Seems like you're curious about a lot, my dear." Then, she turned and walked out the door with a little wave through the window as she went down Main Street.

I shivered as I sat back down in the chair by the art books and texted Mart to explain the orange thing and the gift.

My wise friend wrote back immediately. *You better Google her.*

Right. On it.

I knew I was in for a surprise when Google auto filled *Divina Stevensmith* after I'd typed simply *Divina*. A quick scan of the listings showed she had pieces in galleries from coast to coast, including one of my favorites in Sausalito, California. She's had exhibitions at the MOMA in New York, and she had a permanent gallery down in Salisbury. She was a big deal.

I scrolled through a few listings, looking for anything I could about her personal life. I felt kind of nosy, but I couldn't help it.

Twenty minutes later, though, and I still knew almost nothing about her. She had been born in Baltimore in 1938 and lived in rural Maryland. That's all any site listed. She and her agent – the only person I could find any contact information for when it came to her work – kept a tight lid on her private life. I respected that and was impressed. In this social media age, it took a special prowess to stay out of the headlines, even if you weren't a famous artist.

I spent the rest of the afternoon sending a second round of press releases about the art auction in between ringing up the customers who came in. Cate got Ms. Stevensmith's permission to take a photo of a corner of the piece she was donating so that I could put it on the impromptu webpage I'd created for the fair on our store website. I also added a contact form with the hopes that most of the requests for more information would come through email since I much preferred email to the phone. Finally, I altered the store voicemail to give a bit of background about the street fair and the silent auction and pointed callers to the website.

Then I braced myself for the onslaught of calls . . . that never came. All through Wednesday evening and into Thursday morning, the phone rang only a couple of times with people looking to order particular books. Normally, I would have been thrilled to have orders coming in, but in this situation, I was just disappointed. I had thought Divina Stevensmith's donation would cause a buzz.

In an effort to distract myself and lift my mood, I texted Cate late Thursday morning and asked if she wanted to get lunch. Mart was in town and had offered to come cover the shop for me so that I could get a break. She knew I was sad that the news of the auction hadn't caused more of a stir. While we had eaten frozen pizza and drunk boxed wine the night before, she'd said, "Tomorrow, I'm coming in and working the register so you can get things prepped for the weekend and – and this is non-negotiable – take a few hours away from the store. You've been there all day almost every day since opening. It's time you relaxed for a bit."

Part of me felt guilty – felt like I should be the one giving Mart some time off. She worked so hard, and she was supporting me financially at the moment. But then, she reminded me that her job usually enjoyed a wine tasting a day in some of the most beautiful places in the mid-Atlantic, and I acquiesced.

Cate texted back immediately and suggested we meet at noon at Dale's Seafood Shack. *Then, I'll get Lucas to give you the deluxe tour of the Museum.*

That would be great. See you there at noon.

I had to admit that Mart was right. I really did need a little time away. Between the work to get the shop open, the first few days of business, and then the two murders, I was pretty worn down. It was too early in my business career for me to be feeling that way, and an afternoon in the warm sun of a spring afternoon seemed like just what I needed.

Dale's Seafood Shack was the quintessential Eastern Shore seafood place. Very casual, but with views of the water that you'd pay a fortune for in the city. I'd long ago learned that just because I didn't eat seafood didn't mean that I wouldn't love these places. Cate and I got a table on the covered deck overlooking the river that opened up onto the Chesapeake Bay. I ordered a burger and fries covered in Old Bay, and Cate got a crab cake covered in melted cheese. She also took the liberty of ordering each of us a bottle of Maryland's own Natty Boh beer. The air was still cool, so we had the entire deck to ourselves. It was the perfect way to unwind.

As we sipped our beers, I caught her up on the history I'd learned about the store building. "I never knew any of that."

"Yeah, it feels weird that such an important piece of St. Marin's history isn't noted with a marker or something. I'm definitely going to put something up on the shop and maybe talk to the historical society."

"Good plan. Maybe we can have something temporary printed for Saturday, even a one-page hand-out. Our printer down in Salisbury could do something, I bet. Send me some text, and I'll call him when I get back to the co-op later."

"Oh, thanks. That would be perfect. It's the least we can do to honor Divina's husband."

"Exactly. Plus, it wouldn't hurt as publicity for the shop either."

"True." I felt my concerns about the weekend climb my ribs. "Speaking of which, I haven't had a single query about the silent auction. Don't you think that's odd?"

Cate gave me a mischievous grin. "The ways of Divina have finally reached you. I take it you now know she's kind of a big deal."

"Kind of? She's the biggest kind of deal."

"Exactly. I saw what you put up on your website – well done – but I'm sure her agent has made it clear to the press that all queries are to go through her. Information management. Divina has been especially wily about not letting most of the world know she lives here in St. Marin's."

"But she has a booth at the co-op."

"She does. But she's not on our website, and she doesn't let us advertise her stuff. It's kind of brilliant actually. When people who know her work stumble upon her studio, they are elated, but then, she's quick to draw them in and remind them that her work thrives when she has her privacy. So far, no one has wanted to risk her art for a bit of fame for themselves."

I gave Cate a skeptical glance. "No one? Come on. Not a single person has Instagrammed her shop door and tagged it as St. Marin's."

"Not yet. She's a persuasive woman, and I think people like feeling as if they're part of her inner circle somehow."

I shook my head. "The ways of celebrity will never make sense to me." I looked out over the water and then back at Cate. "But her gift is so generous. I can't believe she'd give something that valuable."

"Why not?" Cate said as she shoved a fry into her mouth. "After all, she can always create more of her work. Plus, she is really devoted to the town. She's funded the park over at the other end of Main Street from you. Paid for an empty lot to be cleaned up and then for the safest, but most fun, playground equipment to be put in. She is a big supporter of the Museum, too."

I was impressed. I liked a story of generosity that didn't come with a lot of accolades. Those gifts seemed more genuine somehow than those that came with the insistence of a name on a building. I really hated the way even all the sports stadiums had become corporate marketing tools. Ravens Stadium was just fine with that name . . . but now some bank paid to have its logo on the building. Ick.

Cate leaned forward a bit as we finished up our beers. "Any more word on Elle?"

It took me a minute to figure out what Cate meant, but then I shook my head. "Nothing. I haven't seen her since we talked to her a couple of days ago."

"I still think she's good for it." Cate sounded like a detective from one of the *NCIS* franchises, maybe that woman in LA with the long dark hair.

"Maybe." I didn't really feel like hypothesizing that my new neighbor was a murderer. "I guess you never know."

We paid our bill, and Cate texted Lucas to let him know we were headed over to the museum. I'd been wanting to go there since I'd moved into town five months earlier, but I had just been too busy.

Lucas met us at the door and gave us the tour through all the exhibits. I had no idea there was such a rich history of watermen. I loved looking at the photos of the old timers out on boats that looked barely watertight but that brought in thousands and thousands of dollars' worth of some of the world's best seafood. Plus, I loved the special exhibit of maritime art. The paintings of water scenes weren't quite as good as the real thing, but if you couldn't live on the water, the best ones made it feel like you could taste the air.

Next, Lucas walked us out to the shipyard, where local artisans were crafting − with old-fashioned tools − a traditional tall-ship, complete with masts carved from single pine trunks. Just now, the workers were hand-hewing the planks to cover the exterior of the ship's hull. It was a laborious and grueling task to build each ship, I could see that, and it made me want to watch even more of those treasure-hunting shows, not just for the treasure now, though, but to recover some of the labor these people had put into these beautiful vessels.

"This is amazing, Lucas. Thank you for the tour," I said as we headed back toward the main building.

"My pleasure. Come back anytime. I've gotten you a member-ship, so just wander over when you need a break." He handed me a little card with my name on it, and I smiled.

"Oh my word. Thank you so much. I'll be back for sure. I need to go see that oyster shack." I gave Lucas a hug. "Oh, and if I send over a list of maritime titles for the new section I'm adding to the store, would that be okay? I don't want to impinge on the gift shop here, but I would like to honor this history in the shop for sure." I'd been resistant to the idea of going too "on brand" for the store, especially since Lucia Stevensmith had made the suggestion, but now, it felt like I was just honoring the stories of this place. I liked that.

"Absolutely. Maybe we can even do an event together sometime? You sell the books, and we get the ticket proceeds."

"Ooh, I love that. Let's make that plan."

He gave us a hearty wave as we walked back up to Main Street. Cate said, "Soon, you're going to have events coming out your ears."

"Actually, I'd love that. Those kind of things bring new people to the store, and while I love St. Marin's, I can't sustain the shop on the number of books people here buy."

"Right. Well, this weekend should help . . . and it looks like you've got buy-in from the other shops in town."

My mind flashed back to Max Davies' and his weird concern about becoming a target. I told Cate about our conversation, still befuddled by his fear.

"Max is an odd one, for sure. But maybe he's afraid of some-thing else."

I turned to look at my friend as we walked into the street. "What do you mean?"

"I mean, maybe he's afraid all those people might suss out what he did."

I chuckled. "So now you think Max Davies is the murderer? Is there anyone you don't suspect?"

She gave my hand a playful slap and said, "Well, you . . . at least not yet."

When I got back to the shop that afternoon, the place was full of people quietly reading or sipping coffee. Mart gave me a wave from the register as I came in and gestured toward the fiction section, where Sheriff Mason was reading the back cover of an Inspector Gamache mystery. "Didn't take you for a police procedural kind of guy, Sheriff."

"You know, I'm probably not. Somehow, reading about a murder in a small town isn't really appealing just now." He carefully slid the book back into its spot and aligned the spine with the rest of the shelf. "Maybe when I retire though."

"If I didn't know better, I'd say you'd worked in a bookstore before." I gestured toward the tidy shelf.

"Right about now, I'd take the quiet of books," he looked toward the storeroom door, "although it hasn't exactly been the easiest of openings for you, huh?"

I shrugged. "Not really, I guess, but even when I think I just want to recommend books and spend time reading, I find that I get into something else anyway. This time that something else just found me." I puffed out my cheeks and blew a long stream of air. "Did you need something?"

"Just wanted to give you a quick update. But before I tell you what I know, I need you to understand something. I'm only telling you all this so that you don't try to snoop it out yourself. I'm hoping that if I satisfy your curiosity, you'll take a step back and just let us do our jobs." He raised his eyebrows and looked at me.

I gave him a small nod.

"Okay then. We did find Stevensmith's hair on the handle of the umbrella, so it looks like it was the murder weapon."

I shuddered. I had held that handle.

"Any fingerprints?"

He scrutinized my face. "No. Nothing usable. And nothing particularly unique about the sage ash either."

My shoulders dropped. "We're no further along than we were."

"The *police* are no further along than *we* were, Harvey. I know you want to help, but you are not a part of this investigation." His voice was kind but forceful, and I felt color run up my neck.

"I'm sorry." I let out a long sigh. "I feel kind of helpless, though. These people died at my shop, and I feel responsible somehow, like I need to do right by them." I slid my hands through my hair. "Plus, I'm just a really curious person. My mom used to say I was a Nosey Nellie, like that girl on *Little House on the Prairie.*"

The sheriff put a hand softly on my shoulder. "I wouldn't say you're anything like snooty Nellie Oleson. And curiosity is a good thing. But Harvey, in this case, you could be putting yourself in real danger."

I knew that all too well, but apparently I didn't seem to care. I did care, however, that I not make things harder for the sheriff. "I hear you. I'll stay out of things and just share information that might come to me." He gave me a stern look. "You have my word that I won't go looking."

He gave my shoulder a squeeze and turned toward the door. "Thanks, Harvey. Glad you're here."

I waved as he headed out to his patrol car. I was glad I was part of this town, too, but I'd be even happier when *they* caught the murderer.

Even though Mart was there to walk home with me, Daniel and Taco still showed up right on time to join the entourage back to the house. Daniel always smelled just a little bit like motor oil and cedar, and tonight, the odor was even stronger. Leave it to Mart to leave no sensory experience unnoted. "Do a little slip-sliding in an oil slick, my friend?" she asked as she slipped her arm playfully into his.

He shrugged, but I saw pink tinge his ears. "I lost my grip on an oil pan under a Dodge 1500 and got soaked. Guess my shower with Lava soap didn't cut it, huh?"

"I like it," I said quietly as I slipped my hand into his. I saw the color in his ears deepen.

Mart chattered away while we walked, and I loved it. She made sense of the world by talking, so I'd long ago learned she didn't need – and sometimes didn't even want – my responses. She was quite content to fritter on while Daniel and I walked quietly and enjoyed the cool evening.

At the door, Mart slipped inside with Mayhem, giving me a wink as she went. Daniel and I stood on the small front stoop under the old-fashioned barn light and just looked at each other. "I could get used to this," he said.

"Me, too." Then, he leaned down and kissed me softly.

I took a step back to head toward the house and fell as Taco's long sausage of a body took me out at the knees. I landed with a thud and just enough sense to catch my head before it smacked the concrete.

Daniel knelt down quickly with a look of great concern on his face. My tailbone definitely hurt, and I suspected I'd have quite the neck ache in the morning. But I started to snicker and then laugh until I was crying and rocking back and forth as I tried to catch my breath.

Eventually Daniel sat down next to me and waited for me to settle. When I could talk again, I said, "You better get used to that, too. I'm not the world's most coordinated person."

"Me neither. Like my new cologne, Eau de Pennzoil?" Then, he laughed so hard his shoulders shook.

Chapter Ten

I was right. My neck was so stiff from my fall that when I woke up, I could only tilt my head but not turn it. I'd been here before. Too many hours reading books in awkward positions had led me to stiff necks many times. I recalled a tip that author **Laraine Herring** had shared at a book reading for her novel *Ghost Swamp Blues*. She said that for a stiffness, you needed to move that body part a hundred times in every direction. It had worked for me before, and I sure hoped it would work again. I had a lot to do and no time to have to rotate my entire body every time I had to make a turn.

I started by doing simple head turns while I was in the shower. The hot water helped, and by the time I'd turned a hundred times in each direction, I was beginning to feel the muscles give. Then, while I made Eggo waffles – the whole wheat ones because I wasn't entirely a lost cause when it came to my health – I tried to put my ears to my shoulders over and over again. Then I did forward bends and pointed my chin to the ceiling. By the time I put on my coat to head out the door, I could turn to call Mayhem without feeling like someone had rammed a hot poker down my back. *Thank you, Laraine.*

And I was so glad I could move when I got to work because

there was a line. A veritable LINE at the door of my bookshop. Rocky was standing just to the side of the door with what I imagined was the same expression I was wearing – one of stupefied glee.

"Any idea what's up?" I asked as I sidled up to her.

"None. But I didn't want to go in without you. These folks look, um, hungry."

She was right. People were shifting from foot to foot and looking at their watches over and over again. A couple of folks were scanning the crowd looking, presumably, for me.

I looped my arm through Rocky's and said in a deep voice, "We're going in."

She squeezed my arm against her. "Aye, Aye, Captain."

Then we gently bumped the crowd out of the way, unlocked the door, slid through, and shut it tightly behind us. I felt like I was trying to keep Aslan in when there was a squirrel in the front yard. I almost had to shove one woman's rubber-booted foot out of the door.

"Gracious," Rocky said as she hurried over to the café. "I'll get the extra carafe going."

"And I'm going to do a quick Google search to see if I can figure out what's up."

It took a scan of only the first three results from my search of "All Booked Up St. Marin's" to see that the buzz had been caused by a post from our friend Galen Gilbert, who was apparently a Bookstagrammer with a HUGE following. On Wednesday, he'd posted a picture of his bookstack that he'd picked up here in the shop, and then yesterday, he'd featured a photo of the shop with a blinking arrow and the words "Go HERE NOW!" on it. I clicked over to his profile and saw he had 86.7K followers. I was dumbfounded. He seemed so unassuming, and maybe that was his charm. Whatever got him those numbers, I needed to know his secrets . . . and I needed to thank him.

Clearly at least a couple dozen of his followers did exactly what he said, and here they were, in the flesh and eager.

I texted Mart, who was planning to head to a local winery this afternoon but was sleeping in this morning. *I need help. Big crowd at door. Come now!!!!*

Her reply came three seconds later. *Baseball cap it is. I'll text Daniel and be there in ten.* Gracious, she was a good friend.

I prepped the shop, got the thumbs-up from Rocky, and opened the door. Now, this wasn't exactly the kind of frenzy that happens when they have those wedding dress sales at those big New York boutiques, but for a small bookstore that had been only open two weeks, one person waiting at the door would have been a thrill; twenty-eight people at the door felt like a miracle.

The book lovers filed in and headed out across the store. I could see that fiction was a big hit, and someone went right to our small drama section. Children's books garnered a few visitors, and a couple of folks went right for the caffeine – I admired their focus and did the same quickly before what I hoped would be a long day of selling books.

Soon, Mart arrived with Daniel and Taco close behind. When I saw the look of relief on his face as he took note that I was fine and even smiling, I realized that Mart hadn't explained very well the nature of the situation. "Sorry she scared you," I said as he leaned on the counter beside me.

"All she said was that you needed help. She was practically jogging here, so I figured it must have been a crisis." He looked around. "Now I see you do need help, just not the way I thought."

I gave his shoulder a bump. "Mart can be a little too enthusiastic sometimes."

"Ah, that's a good quality in a friend. Glad you're alright." He undid Taco's leash, and the Basset headed out to find Mayhem, who had already staked her claim on the big pillow by the history section. "Okay with you if I stay and help out? Fridays are my light days."

"Sure. But really? Fridays are light?"

"Yep. Most of the locals head out of town for the weekend on Fridays if they don't want to manage the tourist traffic."

I frowned. "But the tourist traffic is what keeps the town going."

"Oh, absolutely. I didn't say they didn't like the tourists, but most of us would rather not be in the crowds unless we're working."

I guess that made sense. After all, I was already feeling a little possessive about our little community. I didn't know if I loved the idea of all these outsiders coming in . . . at least I didn't know if I liked that personally. As a business woman, I loved the idea. "Ah, yes, I get that. Well, today I'm working – and, if you're serious, so are you." He nodded, and I put him to work. "Could you go get me some more paper bags from the storeroom? I think I'm going to need them."

Since the initial inflow, the stream of customers into the store hadn't let up. This was clearly our busiest day yet, and it didn't show any signs of slowing down. I handed the register over to Mart and began a sweep of the store – picking up forgotten coffee mugs and reshelving books as fast as I could.

Before I knew it, it was noon, and Rocky was swamped in the café. I trundled over to help her, and she pointed to the back room. "More sandwiches in the fridge . . . and bring all the pastries."

I glanced at the case. It was almost empty. We needed ALL the scones.

By mid-afternoon, we'd found a rhythm. I floated, answered questions, and restocked the bookshelves and the pastry case. Mart ran the register and answered the phone to take special orders, which she jotted down on an Easter Bunny notepad she'd unearthed from somewhere. Daniel helped carry boxes of books out of the back room and kept Mart in change – even though that required not just one, but two, trips to the bank. It was my biggest sales day yet, and I had Galen Gilbert to thank.

I took a minute to message him on Instagram. "Thank you, Galen. Your message has been a huge hit. Look at this." Then I snapped a picture and sent it over.

His reply was almost instantaneous. "Well, I know a good thing when I see it. There are other ways besides murder to drum up business, my dear. See you Tuesday." He'd followed his message with a series of winky-face emojis, and I couldn't help but laugh. People are not always what they appear to be.

By early evening, the crowd had started to thin as we suggested restaurants in town and even a few places to stay. Folks who had never been to St. Marin's before were enamored of the place, and when they heard about Sunday's Street Festival, they were loath to go home. "Why not make a weekend of it?" was a phrase I heard more than once.

Just as we were about to close, a tall, lean, black man came into the store. He stood just inside the doorway for a long time and looked around. Something about the way he studied the space made me wonder if he was remembering, and I thought of Berkeley Hudson and his gas station.

"Thanks so much for visiting All Booked Up. Can I help you find something?"

He looked down at me and blinked a couple of times. "Oh, thank you. I'm actually not here to buy books. I hope that's okay."

I smiled. "Of course, it's okay. Is there something else I can help you with?"

He gazed out over my head into the store. "It's just good to see the place again."

"Again? You've been here before?" I didn't quite know how to ask about Berkeley Hudson since I didn't want to seem like the dumb white lady who assumed all black people knew each other. But I forged ahead. "You came when it was a gas station?"

He smiled down at me. "You know about the station? And about Berkeley, I presume?"

I nodded. "I just learned about the station and how it was a safe haven of sorts, this building and the Hudson house I mean."

He folded his long frame and sat down on the edge of the window display. "My granddaughter sent me the picture she got from one of those online things, said she thought it was the gas station I always talked about. Sure enough, it was." He kept looking out over the room.

"If you told your granddaughter about the station, it must have been important to you." I didn't want to be nosy or push, but he seemed to want to talk, to know it was still safe to share here.

"The most important . . . and also the saddest." He looked me in the eye and raised one eyebrow. "You know the whole story of Berkeley?"

"Um, probably not. I just know he owned the gas station and that he and his wife Divina let people stay with them when they came to town." I felt myself leaning forward, aching to know everything, but this was the kind of curiosity the sheriff had warned me about.

His face softened. "Ah, Divina. What a lovely woman. She still around?"

"Oh yes. Still here in St. Marin's for sure. I expect she'd love to hear from you if you felt like calling on her."

His face grew sad then, so sad that I felt like crying. "I'm not so sure about that. I bring a whole lot of hard memories with me, things she'd probably like to forget."

"Oh." I didn't quite know what to say to that, so I just let the silence rest there a minute. Finally, I said, "Would you like to walk around? You're welcome to go wherever you wish."

He stood up and walked toward the back of the building, then turned and looked out the front window. "The oil cans were kept right there. And he had a display of Michelin tires in that corner. A Pepsi machine over there . . . and he always kept a bag of salted peanuts so we could all drop our peanuts in those Pepsi and have us a good ole snack."

"Peanuts in Pepsi? Like *in* it?"

He chuckled. "Girl, you haven't lived until you've had that goodness."

"I'll have to take your word for it." I grinned.

He was smiling as he looked over the shop, but then that sadness crossed over his features again. "The bathrooms still here?"

"Yep. In the same place, but now they open from the inside of the store. You're welcome to use—"

"No, ma'am. I don't need to go in that room no way, no how. Thank you kindly, but no thank you." He looked almost frightened.

I didn't know what to say, so I just blurted out the first thing that came to mind. "I'd like to know Berkeley Hudson's whole story. I'd like to honor him well in this place. I'm Harvey Beckett. I own the shop here."

When I shook his hand, I noticed how soft his palms were and how long his fingers. "Ralph Sylvester. I was the last man to see Berkeley Hudson alive."

I felt my breath catch in my throat, and then we made our way back to the window display. "I'm sorry. Did you say you were the last person—"

"To see Berkeley Hudson alive. Yes, I did. I was there when they murdered him. Right back there, in the men's bathroom."

I felt faint. Another murder in my shop. "He was murdered here. Oh my goodness. When?"

"1958." His voice was soft, but firm. "The Klan got him."

I sucked in my breath. "The Ku Klux Klan? What?!"

The shrillness in my voice drew his eyes to mine. "Yep, they're the ones. Hoods, burning crosses . . . same everywhere, I expect."

I couldn't even begin to fathom a Klan murder, much less a Klan murder in my shop. But now that I knew a bit, I needed to know it all. "Would you tell me the story?"

He put a hand over mine. "It's a story that needs telling, though it's hard."

I nodded.

"It was April, a beautiful spring. Warm but not humid. Perfect weather for sitting out with a picnic. I remember it was a Saturday because Berkeley and Divina had been over at the town park doing just that while I minded the station."

"About dusk, they were walking back to the station when a whole gang of Klansmen on horseback came into town. I saw them coming from the station window, but I couldn't get to Berkeley in time. Normally, the Hudsons were very careful about being out in public, what with miscegenation laws and everything. But they couldn't resist on this gorgeous day, and the wrong person had spotted them in the park, asked the Klan to send a message."

I felt the tears pushing against the back of my eyes, but I willed them down. This story didn't need my tears, only my ears.

"Berkeley pushed Divina into some bushes next to the garage there." He pointed over to the alleyway between the shop and the hardware store next door. "Then, he ran as fast as he could for the front door. I was ready. Ready to lock the door behind him and head out the back door as fast as we could go. But they got him first . . ." he grew quiet.

"Oh my word." My voice was shaking.

"They took him around back . . . and I found him after I heard them ride off. There was nothing I could do, so I just sat with him until he passed."

I put my hand on Mr. Sylvester's knee. "I don't even know what to say."

He placed his other hand over my own. "There are no words." He took a long, slow breath, and then, his eyes met mine again. "But thank you for letting me share the story."

"Of course. And any time you want to come and be in this space, you are welcome. Any time."

He stood up, and I rose with him. "Thank you for telling me that story, Mr. Sylvester. I'm horrified, but also honored to carry it with me." I looked up at him, and a soft smile crossed his lips.

"I think he'd like that a bookstore was here . . . and you even got the smell of gasoline and clove cigarettes out," he said with a small chuckle.

"Lysol and candles make a great combination."

He looked out over the store again and then turned toward the door. "Thank you, Ms. Beckett. I'll be seeing you."

I scanned the store quickly as he left, and seeing it was empty, locked the door behind him and slid to the floor against it, sobbing.

A few minutes later, someone knocked gently on the glass above my head, and I turned, expecting to see Daniel. Instead, Marcus's concerned face looked back at me. "You okay?" he mouthed.

I nodded and unlocked the door.

"I saw you sitting there and thought you might be hurt." Marcus' jaw was tight with worry.

"Oh, thank you for checking on me, Marcus. I'm okay. Just a hard day. Lots of sad news."

He looked down at his feet. "Yeah, lots of sad things these days."

I didn't know if I had the energy to have yet another intense conversation, but Marcus looked like he needed to talk. So I slid down to the floor again, and he sat down in front of me.

"Marcus, you can tell me to mind my own business, but I'm kind of worried about you."

He looked up sharply. "You don't need to worry about me, Ms. Beckett. I'm just fine. You got enough worries without adding me to the list."

This kid. "Okay, so tell me about you. Where do you come from? What do you do with your time, besides read really great books, I mean?"

He smiled. "I'm from here in St. Marin's actually, but my family hasn't lived here in a while. Mom and I moved away a while back."

"Oh, that's right. You said your mom was an English teacher. Did she teach here?"

He nodded but wouldn't meet my eyes. "For a while."

I leaned forward and caught his gaze. "Marcus?" I didn't want to push, but sometimes, a little nudge was all someone needed to feel heard.

"That reporter that got killed?" His voice was tight, and his jaw hard. Maybe this was the anger Lucas had noted.

Suddenly, I remembered the newspaper article about the teacher and the Little Free Library. "Oh, Marcus, Lucia Stevensmith wrote those horrible things about your mom. I'm so sorry."

"You know about that?" He seemed wary, ready to bolt.

I sat back. "I do. I was doing some research into the murder, and I read the article. It was so unkind . . . your mom had done a wonderful thing, and that woman—" I couldn't finish the sentence because I was too angry.

"Yeah," Marcus said. "She quit teaching after that. We moved over to Annapolis so she could start over as a librarian."

I was grasping at hope anywhere I could get it. "Does she like being a librarian?"

"I think so." There was some life in his voice again. "She loves helping people find books, and story time is her favorite. Plus, the library system is paying for her to get her Master's. She loves that."

"But I bet she misses teaching, too?" I couldn't imagine what it would feel like to be chased away from a job you loved, and this woman had obviously loved her job. You didn't build a Little Free Library for the kids you taught if you didn't have passion for what you did.

"Yeah, she does. But she's okay. Really."

"And are you okay?" I thought for sure I saw tears well up in his eyes, but he straightened up and looked away quickly.

"Yeah, yeah, I'm okay. Still trying to get my feet under me after moving back, you know, but I'm okay. I appreciate the work you've given me, Ms. Beckett. It helps."

I smiled. "Well, I appreciate the work you've done here, Marcus. In fact, if you'd like to work here part-time, I could really use the help." I hadn't been planning on bringing on part-time help so soon, but I needed it . . . and it looked like Marcus needed it, too.

He looked at me warily. "I don't want no pity job, Ms. Beckett."

"It's not pity, Marcus. Have you seen how busy we've been the past few days? Between those two online posts that bring in the book lovers and the two murders that bring in the looky-loos, we are slammed. I would love the chance to get away from the register more and talk to people. If you worked for me, I could do that . . . and you'd get the hefty fifty percent discount on all the books in the store."

"Wait, what?! Working here comes with a discount? Alright then, when can I start?" He was grinning like he was kidding, but I knew – any book lover appreciates a good discount on books.

"How about tomorrow? We open at ten, so be here at nine-thirty."

He jumped up. "Absolutely. Thanks, Ms. B. Is it alright if I call you Ms. B?"

"I'd love that. I've never had a nickname, well, except for Harvey, of course."

"I've been meaning to ask—"

I turned him toward the door. "Another time I'll tell you the whole story. Tonight, you go get some food," I handed him a twenty, "and get a good night's sleep."

His eyes darted down to his feet for just a second before he looked back up. "Thanks, Ms. B."

I paused. "Marcus, do you have a place to sleep?"

He looked down again, and I thought of all the paper towels. He'd been washing up in the bathroom. Why hadn't I figured that out before?

"That's it. Give me my money back."

His eyes got really wide, and he held the twenty out to me limply. "I'm sorry, Ms. B."

"Oh, stop it." I glanced out the window and saw Daniel and Taco waiting. "We're all going to get dinner, and then you'll stay with Mart and me tonight. Tomorrow, we'll make a plan to get you a place."

"I can't do that—"

"You can, and you will. Listen, you don't know me well yet, but I'm stubborn, and I like to be helpful. So let me help. It'll make me feel good."

He grinned then. "Thank you, Ms. B."

"Truly, my pleasure. Now, go tell Daniel that we're going to dinner at Chez Cuisine. My treat."

The bell rang, and I jogged through the shop, turning off lights, checking the doors, and arming the alarm. This might have been the most emotionally grueling day of my life, but something told me, I probably shouldn't say such things.

Chapter Eleven

By the time we opened the next day, we'd arranged to have Marcus move into the room above Daniel's garage. It had, apparently, been a studio apartment at one time, so it just needed some appliances, a little repair to the floors and walls, and a good cleaning to be a perfect apartment for a twenty-year-old man. It took some convincing to get Marcus to agree to take the apartment rent free for the first month, but when Daniel pointed out that his rent would be sweat equity in fixing the place up, Marcus finally said yes.

He even started talking about getting a cat since he'd been so enthralled with Aslan at our place the night before. She had also been quite taken with him and had given up her spot at my feet to set up shop on the guest room bed with him. In the morning, when I peeked in, she had wiggled her way up to the pillow and was draped across Marcus's forehead. If his snore was any indication, he didn't mind at all.

But we didn't have time this weekend to move Marcus in . . . the aftereffects of Michiko Kakutani's tweet combined with the response to Galen Gilbert's Insta post were still sending book buyers from all over Maryland, Virginia, and Delaware. And the murder tourists – who knew there was such a thing? – were still coming, too. Plus, now, we added the people who had come to town for the street fair . . . and we were slammed. Lines at the register, five pots of coffee by eleven a.m. Rocky had to ask her mother Phoebe to come help, we were so busy.

It was amazing.

Marcus took to the register like a champ and was chatting with customers all the while he scanned books. If I hadn't known better, I'd think he'd been doing this for years. Mart was on hand to help with bagging and to take over if he needed to walk a customer to a particular book recommendation. I'm pretty sure he hand-sold more than a few dozen books that day.

I had my handy people counter out again, and by noon, we'd had 743 people in the store. Every seat was taken at almost every minute, and Rocky and Phoebe were doing a brisk business of customers both in the café and with take-out cups. I was very glad Phoebe had come in and also that I'd asked Woody if he could be on call to help out as needed. Turns out our need involved more paper cups, so he contacted the Baptist church down the street and asked if we could buy theirs. The pastor donated them, said she was happy to help support the local bookstore and would replace the church's supply with her own money. I loved this town more and more.

Daniel had a full slate of customers of his own that day, but he did drop by just after lunch to marvel. "Whew! Look at this place."

I took the minute to sit down in the chair I'd tucked in the store-room first thing that morning just so that all of us could get a break for a few minutes at a time. I still didn't love this room, but it was the only private space in the shop, and with this many customers, we needed a little private space. "I know! It's amazing, but holy cow do my feet hurt."

I was wearing my trusty Danskos, which my forty-four-year-old feet appreciated, but even their mighty arches weren't enough to keep the ache away altogether. I'd been walking customers to and fro all morning and bringing out new titles or replacement copies in every spare minute. I was glad I'd ordered a lot of books for the week and super grateful to have the cash to do that.

Daniel sat down on a stack of boxes next to me. "I think we can safely say that your store is officially viable."

"You think?" I laughed, but inside, I was profoundly grateful. The kindness of strangers . . . it was an expression I'd heard a lot, but now I was on the receiving end of it. I felt humbled and even more determined than ever to make this shop do its good work.

I could hear the sound of conversation through the door. "Thanks for stopping by." I gestured toward the door. "I probably need to get out there."

"Oh right. Definitely. But before you go, I almost forgot the second reason I stopped by."

I turned to look at him. "Okay, but first, what's the first reason?"

He put his hand on my cheek. "I think you know that one. But the second one. Max Davis came by. He wanted my opinion on a sound he was hearing in his car, at least that's what he said, but I think he was fishing for information."

"Information about what?"

"Well, that's the thing. He kept talking around something, at least I think so. Said something about us being in the restaurant last night, that maybe I needed to think more about myself and less about helping 'our new neighbor.'"

Our meal the night before had been perfect – crab cakes with remoulade sauce for the guys. A really amazing quiche for me. I think Max had been mortified at my poor taste when I ordered the quiche for dinner. He even came out to suggest the chicken fricassee instead, but I held firm – I wanted cheese and eggs – and he'd relented. It was so good.

"Clearly, he knows I'm a bad influence," I said, trying to make light of the insult.

Daniel laughed, but the chuckle didn't reach his eyes. "He was being casual, Harvey, but I don't think he was kidding. I think he was really trying to warn me off of you."

I felt tears clawing their way up my throat, but I couldn't let Daniel know how much that bothered me . . . or how much I was afraid Daniel would listen. "Is it working?" My laugh came out crackly.

"Not for a second." He leaned down and gave me a gentle kiss. Then he pulled back and looked me in the eyes. "He got me worried, though. I know he and Stevensmith had a falling out . . . do you think he could be the murderer?"

The thought had crossed my mind. Between the very palpable resentment he had about the reporter's reviews and the potential that he might have been faking his paranoia about being a victim at the street fair, I thought it quite possible that he might be our guy. But I still had a question. "Why would he warn you off me, though? What's the value in that?"

Daniel gave me a very serious look and then widened his eyes as if he couldn't believe I wasn't getting it, but I wasn't getting it. "Harvey, he's trying to get me out of the way so he can get to you."

I shook my head. "Nah, that's ridiculous. *Max* is also ridiculous, but he's not dangerous . . . and he's definitely not this conniving."

"You sure about that?" Daniel wasn't convinced, and as confident as I was trying to sound, I wasn't completely convinced either. "At least, make sure you're not alone okay? Keep Mart or Rocky or me nearby."

I wanted to protest, claim my introversion as something that required time alone, but I knew it was better safe than sorry. Plus, I didn't want to worry my friends, at least not any more than they were already. I promised Daniel I wouldn't be alone anywhere but the bathroom, and he thanked me.

But then it was time for me to get back to work. He gave me a quick hug and followed me out the door and back into the shop. I was glad to see the crowd hadn't thinned because I really needed something to distract me from the fact that someone I knew might be out to kill me.

The book buyers kept on coming, and I lost myself in recommending books – Rick Riordan's Egyptian series for a preteen boy who liked reading, but only if it was adventure, then Sarah Vowell's *Wordy Shipmates* for a history buff who appreciated a wry and witty critique, and finally Toni Morrison's *Paradise* to the woman who loved Morrison but only knew her most popular books. *"Paradise* is my favorite. I especially love that it's about a group of powerful women," I said. She bought a copy for herself and one for her best friend.

Between customers, I tried to keep the shelves full – or at least looking so. Our magazine rack looked like a turkey skeleton after Thanksgiving, and the true crime shelves were almost bare. I wasn't sure what I was going to do about inventory for tomorrow's street fair, but when the sun started to set, the crowd thinned out. I thought I'd get a minute to think, but Cate and Lucas came in.

I must have looked about like I felt because Cate gave me a once over, turned to Lucas, and said, "Yep. This calls for soup in a bread bowl."

Just the idea of hot soup and yeasty bread made me salivate. I had never gotten around to lunch, and my body needed nourishment. Nourishment and rest. "That sounds amazing, but I have to figure out what I'm going to do about books for tomorrow. We don't have enough stock to do a bargain table on the sidewalk. I have the 'mystery' books for folks to buy, but the rest of my inventory really needs to stay in here. Otherwise, I'm afraid people will think we're going out of business."

Cate pointed to the chair in the fiction section and gestured for me to sit. Then, she started rubbing her index finger against her thumb while she turned in circles.

"She okay?" I asked Lucas.

He smiled. "Oh yes. This is her thinking ritual."

Cate turned a few more times, and then she stopped and looked at me. "I have an idea."

"See? Told you." Lucas said as he looked from his wife to me.

I laughed. "You two are cute."

They both rolled their eyes, thus confirming my comment. "Okay, what's this idea?"

"Used books."

"But—"

"Before you object. Yes, you are a new book bookstore, but for this purpose, wouldn't it be fun to just have a bunch of miscellaneous books, all for one dollar, let's say. People could pick up titles for themselves, for their friends, for the Little Free Library boxes that are so wonderfully cropping up everywhere."

I considered the idea for a moment. "Okay, I can get on board with that. It does sound fun, but where do we get all these books?"

Lucas laughed so loudly that several people in the shop turned to look at him. "Are you ready?"

"Ready? Ready for what?"

Cate blushed. "Well, I have a basement full of books. Hundreds, maybe thousands of books. I'd love to donate them, maybe have the proceeds go to the scholarship fund?"

I sat up very straight in my chair. "Whoa, whoa, whoa. I have about a million questions. First, you have thousands of books in your basement? How does this happen? I mean I love books, obviously, but thousands? Are they boxed up? On shelves?" I turned my head to look at my friend out of the corner of my eye. "Or is this one of those hoarding scenarios where I'd have to turn sideways and not touch anything lest I be buried alive next to Sasquatch's predecessor?"

"What's this about being buried alive?" Mart's voice was a little high-pitched. I guess even joking about death was a little too close to home right now.

Lucas said, "Harvey is just marveling at the fact that my wife has been accumulating books for decades."

Cate smiled. "*Accumulating* is the nice way of putting it. I adore books, especially art books, and I've never been able to part with a book once I brought it home. So the basement is lined with bookshelves, all sorted by subject."

"And you want to part with them now?" I had a pretty sizable book collection myself – not that sizable but still – and I was very selective about what books I gave away. I loved Cate's idea, but I wanted to be sure she actually loved it.

"I do. Actually, I've been talking about it for a long time. I want to set up a studio in the basement, but I need more natural light. To get more natural light, I need more windows. To get more windows, I have to have walls . . . and right now, every wall is covered with a bookshelf."

Lucas looked at me and said, "It's time. Please, please accept this offer. I'm tired of having to eat dinner on a TV tray because a painting is drying on the dining room table." He got down on his knees and clasped his hands together in front of me. "Take the books, Harvey. Please."

I cracked up. These two people made me very happy. I looked at Cate. "If you're sure."

"Totally." She headed toward the door, and then looked back at Lucas. "You coming? We have books to sort."

"I guess we're leaving, but come by after you close up. I'll have potato soup – with bacon, I presume? – in a sour dough bread bowl for you. You, too, Mart. "

I had loved a lot of things about San Francisco, but soup in a bread bowl – that was one of my favorites. "Yes to the bacon, please," I looked at Mart who was nodding her head like she was one of those bobblehead dolls in the back window of a car on a back road. "We'll see you later," I called after Cate and Lucas.

"My word," Mart said. "So we need to get some tables?"

"Oh crap. I hadn't even thought about tables." Here I was recommending that people put out tables with specials for the fair, and I didn't even have a table myself, much less enough tables to hold hundreds, maybe thousands of Cate's books.

Mart already had her phone out. "No worries. I got this." As I got up to tidy up the store and help Marcus ring up the last few customers, Mart slid into the chair without even looking up from her phone. She had this.

By the time we closed up, we'd had 1,854 visitors to the store – maybe a few more since I was in the back for a bit with Daniel. And a quick run of the register tally showed I'd made more that day than I had in all the days before combined. I was giddy. Giddy and exhausted.

All I wanted was that soup in a bread bowl, a big cup of tea, and my bed. But we still had prep to do for the next day. At least I thought we had prep to do. "Okay, we're all set. Tables, extra coffee carafes, more cups and plates, and a supply of St. Boudreau's best wine will be here at nine a.m. Anything else we need? My boss is happy to help."

I just stared at her for a minute while my brain tried to process what she'd just said. "We're having wine?"

"Yep, I'll be serving as an employee of the winery – just tastings – but we'll have bottles for sale, too. Thought it might get a little more foot traffic."

I felt the smile on my face, and I was very excited . . . but the idea that even more people would be coming to my store left me a little stupefied. The shock slowly gave way to panic. "Mart, where are we going to put all these things?"

"Got that under control, Ms. B," Marcus said as he dropped beside me on the floor. "I did a sketch." He handed me a sheet of printer paper with what looked like a to-scale drawing of the store.

The wine would be in the front of the café against the windows to draw people in but not impede the flow for pastry eaters and coffee drinkers. Then, we'd shift the café tables into the main part of the shop, giving people places to sit and rest with their wine or coffee but also keeping the space open in the café itself. Then, Cate's books would be on long tables all across the front and the side of the store that opened onto a parking lot. Mart had secured permission from the garden center next door to use the edge of their lot since it was a bit early for them to have much merchandise, but they had also assured her that they would do their part and have as many flowering shrubs as they could out on the street to draw people over.

I studied the plan and let out a hard sigh. It was all under control. "Thank you all so much. I feel like I say this all the time, but really, I couldn't do this without you." I blew Rocky a kiss as she and her mom cleaned up the last of the dishes and shut down the café.

I gave everyone hugs as they headed out the door. Mart lingered just long enough for Daniel to arrive, and then she gave Marcus a lift home. He'd be staying with us until he had time to get his apartment ready. "Meet you at Cate and Lucas's?" she said. "You come, too, Daniel. Cate said so."

"Sounds good." He waved as they left, and then looked at me. "What am I doing now?"

"Potato soup in a bread bowl," I said with a smile.

"Oh man, that sounds so good." He pointed to the window display. "You sit here. I'll close up."

I smiled and gave him the alarm code. It felt good to sit down. As Daniel headed toward me across the shop, I heard a knock at the window and turned to see Elle there – her arms full of flowers. I groaned. I had totally forgotten she was bringing those by for tomorrow. I shouted to Daniel and asked him to turn off the alarm, and then I let Elle in.

The flowers were amazing. I had imagined she'd bring me pink and purple flowers – soft pastels – but there were salmon blooms and hot pink ones, too. Even a burgundy and a yellow. "Oh, Elle, I love them. I didn't realize that hyacinths came in so many hues. Thank you."

"You're welcome. I'm sorry I didn't get here sooner. I got caught up with customers all day. Most of them had books, so I think we probably have you to thank for the boost in early-season business."

"It wasn't me. It was Michiko Kakutani and Galen Gilbert and their fans. I can't believe it."

She set the five-gallon buckets full of flowers and water down to the left of the door. "You're being too humble. They praised your shop because it's worth praising. This is a wonderful spot, Harvey."

"Well, thank you, and I am really glad my good fortune is spreading down the street."

"Oh, it most definitely is. I sold out of butternut squash by eleven a.m.. I've never been so glad for my little greenhouse and the fact that peas love cooler weather. I'm glad I ordered extra flowers, too. Lots of folks have spring fever and wanted fresh bouquets. But I held these back . . . just for you."

I looked again at the flowers. "These are amazing. They're a much-needed boost after a whopper of a day."

"Indeed. After the news about the sheriff, we all need a boost."

I clenched my jaw. "The sheriff? What happened?" I looked to Daniel as he walked up and then back at Elle. "Is he okay?"

"Oh," Elle put her hand on my arm, "I'm sorry, honey. I didn't mean to scare you. Oh yes, Sheriff Mason is fine. But someone did slash his tires and paint that horrible word on his patrol car. He was madder than spit when I saw him a few hours ago."

I turned to Daniel. "Oh my goodness. Had you heard about this?"

"Yep. Pretty awful."

I shook my head. "As if he doesn't have enough to deal with, two people murdered including his deputy, and someone wants to stir up racist BS. Unbelievable." I could feel the anger running through my fingers. When I'm tired, my emotions often get the best of me, and tonight I was exhausted. "Does he know who did it?"

Elle shrugged. "He's pretty tight-lipped about most things." She looked down and sighed. Then she met my gaze again. "But he's a force to be reckoned with. I wouldn't mess with him."

I nodded. He seemed mild-mannered, but I imagined that if he needed to be, our kind sheriff could be a hurricane of justice.

Daniel headed back to re-arm the alarm, and Elle and I walked out onto the street. "Thanks again for the flowers, Elle. I'll get you a check once all this slows down, if that's alright."

"Oh, that's fine. We'll all be a little flush with cash after this weekend. Thanks again for this, Harvey. You've really boosted not only our revenues, but our spirits here."

I blushed. "That's kind of you to say. Now, if only we could find the person who murdered Stevensmith and Deputy Williams. It would feel like a good end to a hard couple of weeks."

Elle shrugged. "I guess so. Sometimes, though, I think some questions are best left unanswered, don't you?"

Daniel came out and joined us. "Some questions, yes," he said, "but not a question about murder. All of the questions about a murder need to be solved."

She gave us a thin smile and climbed into her pick-up.

As she drove away, I thought about that stack of newspaper articles on her desk. What had she been trying to answer?

We made it to Cate and Lucas's just as the soup was coming off the stove. It smelled heavenly, like comfort had been made into vapor and spread throughout the room. "Oh, Lucas, I may pass out from delight," I said as I slung my scarf and coat over the nearest chair and fell into it.

"Now, that's a response to my cooking that I could get used to," he said with a small laugh. "I left the bacon out because I wasn't sure if any of you were vegetarian."

"Bring on the bacon," Mart and Daniel said at the same time before both cracking up. We were all a little on edge with all the busyness in the shop and the fair tomorrow and, well, the murders. It felt good to just be silly and indulgent.

"Help yourselves," Lucas said as he gestured to a spread on their kitchen island. Normally, I was the kind of person who prefers to go last, but tonight, I just wanted to eat. I grabbed a plate, a perfect bread bowl – not as huge as those at Fisherman's Wharf in San Francisco but not a dinner roll either – and ladled it full with the thick, white soup. Then, I dropped a good portion of bacon in and covered it all with more than my fair share of shredded cheddar.

Cate had just finished pouring big glasses of ice cold water, so I grabbed one of those and then tucked myself into the far corner of the dining room table by the window. I didn't even mind my manners and wait for everyone to sit. I just dove in. My mother would be horrified.

The table was filled with the sounds of satisfied eating for several minutes until Mart pushed back her plate, leaned back in her chair, and said. "Man alive, did I need that or what?"

I couldn't even find words. I just nodded. I was satiated and relaxed . . . and wiped out. Totally wiped out.

"Oh, did I forget to mention that there's cupcakes?"

Daniel groaned. "If I had known, I wouldn't have had that third bowl of soup."

"I know. That's why I didn't tell you." Lucas grinned. "Besides cupcakes are, as my grandmother always said, highly squishable.

Want me to poke around in your belly like she did just to prove you have room?" He pointed a finger toward Daniel's stomach.

"No, thank you. I fear that I may have more room than intended if you explored." He let out a long sigh. "But I will take a cupcake . . . to honor your grandmother, of course."

"Of course." Lucas got up and came back with a tray of the most amazing cupcakes I'd ever seen. They were huge – the size of those giant muffins you get in some bakeries – and topped with no less than three inches of icing. I immediately spied a white cake with white icing that had my name on it and lunged.

Cate made her move for her cupcake of choice at the same time, and we smacked heads hard just under the chandelier.

I sat back, cupcake in hand, and tried to focus while tears sprang to my eyes. It appeared, however, that Cate had gotten the worse end of our collision because her nose was bleeding . . . and worse yet, it was dripping into her cupcake frosting.

Mart and Lucas sprang into action grabbing paper towels and removing the blemished cupcake before getting Cate to put her head over the back of the chair and applying pressure.

"Oh, Cate, I'm so, so sorry." I felt terrible. "Are you okay?"

She let out a muffled laugh. "Oh yes, I'm just fine. We probably need to call our shots on cupcakes from now on, though. Dessert should not be a full-contact sport."

I still felt awful, but she recovered quickly, claimed another cupcake, and persuaded me to compete in an icing-licking competition with her. We could only lick with a flat tongue. No bites and no deep dives that weren't really licks. The person who lost had to clear the table.

It was a fierce battle, but I was a baked good expert and I finally took her by a few licks. I felt a little light-headed from the blow to the head, my reduced oxygen intake during the competition, and the sugar rush, but I was still having a hard time remembering when I'd had so much fun.

In the end, we all helped Cate clean up and then she showed me her 138 totes of books that she was bringing to sell in the morning. "Cate, woman, how are you going to get all these there?"

"Oh, Woody's coming by bright and early to help us load. We'll be at the shop by eight-thirty or nine to set up . . . unless you need us earlier."

"No, ma'am. After all this work and the fact that I made you bleed tonight before taking your title as Icing Licker Extraordinaire, I wouldn't dare ask for more."

Cate slid an arm around my waist. "Harvey, you're our people. Sure glad you're here."

I smiled all the way to the door, where we all hugged goodbye. I had found my people, and it felt incredible.

Mart, Daniel, the two dogs, and I took the long way home via Main Street. I think we all needed a little time to wind down. The town was quiet. Televisions lit front windows with a blue glow, and, as we passed a couple of houses, the sounds of laughter reached us on the sidewalk. A few cars passed us slowly, no one in an apparent hurry to get anywhere, and while the night was cool, it wasn't cold. In fact, the slight chill felt good against my tired skin.

We didn't talk much except to make sure we all knew our stations for the morning. We had just turned onto Main Street when I saw a moving light behind the art co-op. At first, I thought it was just someone's headlights as they drove through the alley like a lot of folks did to avoid the single stoplight in town. But then, when it slid by my line of vision again, I saw it was a flashlight beam and shook my friends' arms up and down before pointing.

"Look," I whisper-shouted, and we all stopped. Yep, someone was shining a light around behind the co-op like they were looking for something.

I thought of all those TV shows where people are trying to find something in a dark house and shine their flashlights all around as if someone wouldn't notice beams of light in an otherwise dark house. This person had clearly not watched enough television.

Daniel pointed to us and then down the street and then at

himself and toward the co-op. "You want us to walk away and leave you here," I said.

He scowled . . . and then nodded with exaggerated fervor.

"We're three blocks away. I don't think they can hear us."

"Alright." He looked like I'd taken away all the excitement. Maybe he'd wanted to pretend we were special forces or something. "Yes, you guys go down the street and call Sheriff Mason. I'll get a closer look. But here, take Taco. He can't sneak up on dinner."

I wanted to argue, to remind him that the moment when people split up was the moment when the killer got them, but he was already headed toward the alley. At this point, my safest course of action was to call the police, and I didn't want to be overheard . . . even if I did think that was unlikely still.

Mart and I tried to look casual as we walked as fast as we could past the co-op and down to my shop. Then, I dialed 911, told them what we'd seen, that Daniel was checking it out, and that we needed someone as soon as possible.

Then, we stood there, huddled together with the dogs straining to go sniffing down the road. The cold air didn't feel so great anymore.

Just as Sheriff Mason pulled up in what appeared to be his own vehicle, wearing jeans and a T-shirt and looking a little bleary-eyed, Daniel came around the corner of the co-op building with Divina Stevensmith.

"You guys are always in the thick of it, huh?" the sheriff said as Daniel and Divina came down the street.

"It appears that way. But I give you my word that this time, we really were just walking home and saw a light," I said, feeling chagrined no matter the truth of my words.

The sheriff gave me a skeptical look but turned his attention to Daniel and Divina as they reached us.

"I'm so sorry to worry everyone. I just lost one of my good knives out in the back of the co-op sometime recently, and I didn't want to risk it cutting someone at the fair tomorrow."

"What kind of knife was it, Divina? Maybe we can help you

look." I tried to keep my voice calm, but I saw the sheriff cut his eyes toward me.

"Oh, you know, it's one of those pencil-like ones that has a razor blade on the end . . . I think scrap bookers use them a lot."

Ah, so not the knife used to kill Deputy Williams. I was surprised to find I was both relieved and a little bit disappointed. For a minute there, I thought we had a good lead.

"Should we all go look?" Daniel asked, and our little huddle moved back to the co-op and around the building.

None of us but the sheriff and Divina had flashlights, so we used our phones to search the ground. I checked right up against the building with the idea that that kind of thing can easily fall in the transition from outside to inside or vice versa, but didn't find anything.

Then, I started to fan out, searching the lot, including the space where Divina said she usually parked. All of us looked and even wandered into the grass in case a squirrel or crow with a penchant for shiny things had tried to make off with their booty.

We were just about to give up and tell Divina we'd take a sweep again in the morning when she squealed from over by the co-op's back door. "Oh, I found it. It was right here." She pointed to a spot to the left of the door. "Thank goodness. I wouldn't have wanted some child to pick it up and get cut."

I walked over and looked at the knife that was about as long as a ballpoint pen. "So weird. I looked over here and didn't see it." I stretched my back. "But I'm exhausted, so my eyes are a bit wonky."

Divina patted my arm. "You've had a busy few days, and an even busier one tomorrow, I suspect. We best all be getting home. Thank you all for your help and kindness."

She headed to her hot pink Volkswagen beetle and climbed in. "I've always admired that about Divina. She's loaded, but the only sign of that is the custom paint job on her very sensible car," Daniel said.

I shook my head. "Not a color I'd pick." Then I looked at the sheriff. "You know all of us searched that spot by the door, right? That knife was not there."

He looked at me. "I did. I am a trained police officer." He gave me a wink. "But yes, that is odd."

"Maybe she found it in her bag while she was searching and felt embarrassed so she fake-dropped it." Mart didn't sound convinced by her own theory.

"Maybe," the sheriff said with a worried look on his face. "Maybe."

Chapter Twelve

I collapsed into bed as soon as I got home. I was exhausted from work and planning the street fair. But more, I was just worn down by the weight of all this sleuthing. The sheriff must be tired all the time, I thought. I felt Aslan climb up next to me – forsaking Marcus, it seemed – just before I fell asleep.

I felt like I'd only been asleep a few minutes when I wrenched my body over with a start and felt a strain in my shoulder. I was gasping and covered in sweat, and Aslan was sitting at the end of the bed staring at me.

The dream had been so real. I was in the bookstore by myself shelving books and just generally cleaning up after the day when I heard a thud from the back of the store. Thinking Mayhem had knocked a book off the shelf, I casually walked back to pick it up when a hand reached around and grabbed me by the face, silencing me and cutting off my airways all at the same time.

In my dream, I thrashed and kicked and tried to scream, but the person attached to the hand was far stronger than I was. I couldn't get free. They dragged me into the storeroom and locked the door, and when I looked up, it was Lucia Stevensmith. She was clearly still dead, but she was also clearly angry.

"You need to figure out who did this to me. You and your stupid books and your stupid store in this stupid town. Figure it out so you can get out."

Her voice was so angry that it stung. "I'm not leaving St. Marin's, hopefully ever. So I guess you're stuck with me." I was impressed and terrified by my own valor.

Lucia came and stuck a bony finger in my face. "You're digging up stories that needed to stay untold, woman. Stop poking at the past. Let it die. We don't need to dredge up old history."

I stared at her for a long while, and then, she just evaporated . . . and that's when I woke up. I drew Aslan to me and sat snuggling her for a long time, despite her desire to sleep in a ball on the extra pillow. My subconscious was obviously trying to tell me something, but I couldn't put my finger on what about the past I was missing.

My clock said it was two a.m., and I had to be at the store by seven. I'd have to figure out what Lucia didn't want me to put together another time. Now, I needed to sleep, and Aslan agreed. I snuggled back under the comforter, and she rolled over to rest her haunches against the back of my leg. Comforting, if not entirely comfortable.

Later that morning, I awoke to my alarm. My body ached from exhaustion, but my mind was not going to let me sleep a minute past six. We had work to do. I crawled out of bed and made my way to the coffee pot, only to find it was already brewing. I tried to open my eyes enough to look around, but I ran into Marcus, who was sitting at a bar stool with his own cup of joe, reading *Possession*. "Oh, sorry," I said. "You're up early."

"Wanted to get an early start at the shop, but first, I had to read a bit more about what Roland and Maud are finding."

It took me a minute, but then I realized he was talking about the characters in the novel and smiled. "Glad you're liking it, and thanks for planning to come early. We have a LOT of setting up to do."

"No problem. I hope it's okay, but I asked my mom to come by, too." He looked over the top of his book with trepidation.

"Of course it's okay. I'm so excited to meet her . . . but if you'll excuse me, I really need to drink some of this fine coffee you have made, and you have another few pages to squeeze in."

He grinned and tucked his nose back into his book while I dug out the coffee mug I'd won at a college holiday party. It was the size of a large soup bowl, which seemed about right for today.

Mart, Marcus, Daniel, and I were at the shop by seven, a time Aslan even refused to acknowledge with her presence. Mayhem, however, was eager to get out for an early morning sniff-and-pee until we got to the shop, that is. At that point, she climbed onto the tiny dog bed in the window display – meant for a visiting teacup poodle or dog-loving cat – and passed out. Only her chest fit on the bed, so she made quite the sight with her belly up, all four paws in the air, and this little pink pillow below her shoulders. I took a picture and decided it would be the first image on the Instagram page I wanted to create for the shop.

By seven-thirty, Rocky and her mom had arrived with trays and trays of baked goods. "Gifts from the ladies at church," Ms. Phoebe said. "You know those women are always just looking for an excuse to bake."

I laughed and said, "Please thank them for me. You'll keep track of what I owe everyone?"

Phoebe took a step back. "Woman, no. These are gifts. All the money goes to the scholarship fund."

I already felt the tears coming to my eyes, and we hadn't even started the day. "That is so kind. Maybe I could host a women's book club for them here . . . do they like to read?"

She smiled. "Some of them do. But don't tell the preacher, now: most of us love romances."

"You got it, then. A clandestine romance book club that we'll call, "Lovin' On" just to seem holy."

She arched her back and laughed so loudly that I felt it in my throat. I liked this woman.

Outside, Marcus had gotten all the tents set up and had hung two banners that he had ordered the day before on the front and side of the building by the garden center.

"Used Books – $1.00. All proceeds go to the Skye Williams' Scholarship Fund."

In the corner of each banner, there was a small stack of books and a very cute logo for the shop . . . I'd been hoping to design one, but apparently, Marcus had taken care of that for me. I was pretty sure that young man would be the assistant manager here before long.

Up and down the street, I saw the shop owners putting out tables and hanging decorations. The garden center had outdone themselves with the hanging baskets for the street lamps, and the town had offered their employees time and a half if they wanted to work the fair – hanging baskets, emptying trash, answering questions, etc. Already, the street was more full than on a normal Sunday, and we were just the folks working.

I heard the sheriff coming before I saw him. His patrol car was playing "Uptown Funk" over the loudspeaker as he drove into town, and I saw even the most stoic among us start to swing our hips. I was outside helping Cate and Lucas unload their totes of books, and the sheriff stopped and rolled down his window when he saw me.

"You done good, Harvey Beckett. Real good." He grinned. "This is a great day already . . . and I have it on good authority that the weather is going to be perfect." He leaned out of the car window and winked at Woody.

"That's right. Red sky last night . . . sure does look like it'll be delightful. Maybe even hit seventy today."

"Oh, I hope so," I said as I waved to the sheriff's departing car. I was trying to figure out how to best display Cate's beautiful art book collection. "These are incredible, Cate. Are you sure you're okay with parting with them? "

Cate gave me a look that said, "This again."

"Okay. Okay. But really, only a dollar? We could get more for them."

She looked at the books and said, "We could, but we don't need to. And I really like the idea of people who don't have fifty dollars to spend on an art book getting one for just a dollar. I plan on staying here all day and telling people about the artists and answering questions."

"Just don't scare the customers away, my love," Lucas said as he hefted another tote onto a table. "Not everyone wants to know about the reason behind Frida's unibrow."

"Wait, she had that facial hair for a reason? Oh man, I want to know that story, but I have to get inside. I just remembered, I haven't gotten out the mystery books yet. Tell me later?" I waved as I rushed back into the shop.

Inside, I stopped in my tracks when I saw what Mart had done with the front table. It was an entire display of books about segregation and the Jim Crow South, and at the center, she'd placed *The Negro Motorist Green Book*. Its forest-green cover shone like a beacon, and I wondered how people would feel about it. I hoped our black customers would find it honoring, especially given the history of the building. A couple of days ago, I'd looked it up and found that they'd made a reproduction of the 1940 book . . . and Mart had, somehow, managed to get copies to feature here in the shop. I loved that woman.

I couldn't wait to show Divina, and I sure hoped Mr. Sylvester would stop by. I really wanted them to know I'd heard them and was doing all I could to honor the memory of Berkeley Hudson. As I rushed past the check-out counter, I made a quick note to myself so I wouldn't forget to take care of something as soon as the festival ended.

But now, I had to get out those mystery books because I could see the foot traffic outside starting to pick up. I grabbed the box of books from the storeroom, trying not to think about Lucia Stevensmith when I darted in and out – and laid the box on the table for

Mart to sort. "Got it," she said as I sprinted off to check on Rocky and Phoebe.

The mother-daughter team was in full swing with carafes of coffee – dark roast and medium roast in the full-strength kind plus decaf for those who needed it – and a veritable tower of cinnamon rolls. They'd also stocked the pastry case with an assortment of scones and spring-decorated cookies, and I thought I even spied small quiches as I gave them a big thumbs up on my way back outside.

As I darted beneath the ringing bell, I saw Daniel helping Cate and Lucas set out the books, and he gave me a smile that made my heart bounce just a bit. I looked up the street, and the other businesses were pulling out tables and setting up displays as far as I could see. Next door, the garden center had brought out a variety of hydrangea and viburnum. In front of the large shrubs, they placed smaller containers of these flowering bushes that had dark-green leaves and these beautiful purple or white flowers that hung gently from stems. I caught the owner's eye and pointed, "Hellebores," she said. "Lenten rose."

I grinned. I wasn't much of a church-goer myself, but I did know that Fat Tuesday was coming up, and if their name was any indicator, these beauties were blooming right on time.

Marcus, Lucas, Cate, and I spent the better part of the next hour laying out Cate's books, trying to organize them at least a bit into broad categories – photography, painting, sculpture, etc. Fortunately, Lucas was able to convince Cate that we didn't really have enough tables or space to break them down by genre or time period, or else we might have been sorting when the street festival ended.

Finally, about eight-thirty, I told Marcus I needed to check on Divina's art and decided to take the opportunity to walk Mayhem quickly before the crowd really arrived. Although, by the look of Main Street, people were already shopping, and some shop owners looked more than ready to begin their sales. The two older gentlemen who owned the hardware store next to my shop had put out a collection of odds and ends that looked like they could draw in the *American Pickers*. A bit further down the road, I noticed that Max Davies must have over-come his fear because he had a member of his waitstaff outside with coupons for twenty percent off an evening's meal as well as surprisingly cute recipe cards for a chocolate soufflé and his Duck a l'Orange.

The folks at the hair salon were offering discounts on walk-in haircuts that day, and I wished I had time to stop and have my do trimmed. When you have thick curly hair cut short like mine, you can't go too long between trims or you start to look like Lyle Lovett. That guy's music is great, and the hair is great on him . . . not so much on me.

Elle Heron had out vegetable starts – lettuce and broccoli, cabbage, and maybe kale. I never quite understood kale or the rage around it, but she was already doing a brisk business. I gave her a little wave as I passed.

At the co-op, a young man with the largest ear gauges I'd ever seen was just opening the door, and he said, "Ms. Beckett?"

"Yes, that's me."

"Ms. Stevensmith wanted me to let you know that her piece is here and to show you where it is."

"Oh good. Thanks!" I must have looked worried because he gave my arm a little squeeze as he walked past me to lead the way down the hall.

And there it was, right in the middle of the main gallery space at the center of the building. The piece was exquisite – exquisite and huge. It stood almost two stories tall, reaching up to the bottom of the handrail on the second-floor catwalk above. The colors were stunning – all pinks and purples, some gentle blues – all pieces of paper cut and folded to give the appearance of movement.

I knew the piece was a study of our town, a study done in the dark, if the title was literal, and I could see it if I looked hard – the cupola on the top of the courthouse, the jettison roof of the maritime museum, even the thin rails of ship masts lined up at the marina – but the beauty of the piece was that it could be almost anything the viewer wanted to see. One minute, I contem-plated the flower-like appearance of the paperwork, and the next I felt like I was looking at the ocean after a nighttime squall. It was absolutely magnificent, and I found myself unable to move away.

"So you like it then?" Divina said as she came into the gallery and stood beside me.

I looked at her with awe. "Like it? Ms. Stevensmith, it is, it is . . . oh, I don't even have the right words. Incredible, breath-taking, poignant."

She smiled and kept her eyes on her art. "It is one of my favorites." She glanced quickly at me. "I know that probably sounds prideful of me to say, but I've always thought that if an artist doesn't love her work, then how could anyone else?"

I smiled. "I completely agree. And Divina – is it alright if I call you Divina?" She nodded. "Thank you. I'm so grateful for your gift. You didn't have to be so generous."

She smiled and then turned, and I thought I heard her say, "Oh, but I did." But she moved off quickly, so I didn't get to ask her what she meant.

I glanced down at my watch. 8:50. I had to get back. I thanked the man at the desk, untied Mayhem from the light pole outside, and walked as quickly as I could without looking ridiculous. It just wouldn't do for me to be late to my own street fair.

The next two hours went by in a blur. Fortunately, Cate and Lucas had come with a cash box and plenty of change since they were doing a swift business outside, and I couldn't spare a person to help them. Marcus was masterfully handling the Mystery Book table, and when we'd already almost sold out, I sent him to the children's section to get more– "Pick the ones you like." The grin on his face told me he appreciated my trust.

Mart wasn't doing tastings until eleven, but already, she had folks stopping by to ask about the wine and pick up a bottle or two, and when they needed refreshment, they got coffee and a cinnamon roll or scone from Rocky and her mom. Business was brisk, and people were happy.

Meanwhile, I staffed the register and tried to – as politely and clearly as possible – point customers to the right sections for the books they were seeking. When Daniel came in and offered to run the register, I didn't even take the time to ask him if he knew how before I scampered off after a teenage girl who was looking for the new Leigh Bardugo title but was headed right for our small section of erotica.

When Sheriff Mason and his wife, Lu, arrived at noon with a full tray of tacos, I was ecstatic. "Bring me the tacos," I said in a low, growling voice.

The sheriff took a step back in pretend horror, but Lu stepped right forward and said, "I hear that voice. That's the voice of a woman with a business to run. Give that woman a taco, Tuck."

"Yes, ma'am, don't want anyone else getting hurt around here," he said as he leaned over to me with the tray. "Harvey, this is amazing."

I shoved half a taco in my face, and then said, "Thanf oo or uh baffos."

He laughed. "You're most welcome. You eat. I'm going to deliver the rest of these to the crew." He kissed his wife on the cheek and headed out to play waiter.

I finished my taco in record speed and took a deep breath. "Seriously, those tacos are incredible."

"Why, thank you!"

"Wait. I know these tacos. What?! You run the taco truck?!"

"Indeed I do. Lu is short for Luisa. . . as in Luisa's Lunch Luxury." She grinned.

Then, I remembered. That was the name on the taco truck . . . painted in a swirling script above a woman's face, Lu's face I realized. "Well, if I didn't already plan to be in St. Marin's for a very long time, your tacos would be the deciding factor."

Just then, Daniel walked over, a taco in each hand and *the* Taco trailing behind. "Daniel, do you know Lu Mason?"

He looked at his hands and then made quick work of one taco before shaking Lu's hand. "I don't know you personally, but I have eaten many of your jalapeno-chicken tacos. Thank you."

"Ah, yes, the mechanic. My young assistant knows you well." She raised her eyebrows at Daniel, and I felt my heart rate quicken. I had competition.

"Oh yes, I know your assistant. Long blond hair, beautiful brown eyes. About eighteen inches tall."

Lu laughed, but I wasn't getting the joke. "Yes, that's her. Sandy is a sucker for a dark-haired man."

My smile had fallen away, and I was looking from Lu to Daniel and back. Daniel took a step over and stood beside me, letting his arm fall casually over my shoulder. "Harvey's a dog lover, too. That's her girl Mayhem over there with my Taco." He pointed over to the bed beside the fiction section.

Then it clicked. Sandy was a dog. I was fairly sure my face was the color of Lu's enchilada sauce. At least my heart was beating again. "What kind of dog is Sandy?" I asked trying to look like jealousy hadn't been keeping all my synapses from firing.

"Oh, she's a Cocker Spaniel. Spoiled as anything. Every night, Tuck gives her a serving of my tres leches cake. Soon, I'll have to get a cart to carry her because her belly will drag the ground."

Daniel laughed. "She is a little portly."

"A little portly. You are kind. If she gets fatter, she'll be round, and we'll be able to just roll her around town."

I was laughing so hard that I almost didn't notice when Galen Gilbert came in. If he hadn't stopped to pet Mayhem and Taco on his way to the mystery section, I might have missed him altogether.

"It was nice to meet you, Lu. Maybe I can try some of Sandy's tres leches cake some time," I said as I scooted after Galen.

He had already scooped up a handful of mass markets – mostly culinary cozies this time, I noticed. I slipped a copy of Avery Aames *The Long Quiche Goodbye* onto the top of his pile before he noticed me, and when he glanced down, he smiled. "Oh, I love that series." Only then did he look up to see who had placed the book on his teetering stack.

"Harvey. You have good taste in mysteries."

I grinned. "Thanks. I just love a punny title . . . and Providence, Ohio, is one of my favorite towns where people die all the time."

Galen roared. "Yes, goodness, if the murder rates were as high in major cities as they are in these fictional small towns, we'd run out of cemeteries."

"Let me take these for you, hold them at the desk if that's okay?"

"Of course. Thank you."

"No, Galen. Really, thank you. You gave us a huge gift in sharing a piece of your Insta feed with us. Our business has been booming for much better reasons now."

He looked down at the bookshelves again. "It's the least I could do. I want more people to read, and I think small bookshops like yours are part of the key to helping that happen."

"Well, thank you. Now, what brings you to town today? I thought you were a usual Tuesday visitor."

He walked with me back to the counter, where Daniel was managing the line with aplomb. "I am, but I read about the street fair on *your* Instagram feed and couldn't miss it. Besides, on Tuesday, I have to run another errand so can't come then."

His face had grown serious, so I put his books down beside Daniel and took a step closer to Galen. "Everything okay? I mean I don't want to pry—"

His chin shot up, and I saw a glint of mischief in his eye. "Oh yes, I just have a date that afternoon is all."

"A date. Ooh la la. Who's the lucky woman?"

"A Bulldog named Mack."

I cackled. "As in Mack the Mack Truck spokesdog?"

"That's the one. He's at the local SPCA, and I've decided I need a roommate."

"Well, Galen, when Mack is ready for primetime, I hope you'll bring him by."

"Oh, he'll be here for mystery Tuesdays, don't you worry."

I helped Daniel bag Galen's purchases and then told Galen I looked forward to seeing Mack's introduction on Insta. He grinned, winked, and headed toward the door before turning and saying, "Oh, I want to bid on that art piece. How do I do that?"

Daniel stepped forward. "I have to walk that way to get something at my garage. I'll show you . . . besides, I want to take a peek myself." Daniel winked as he held the door open for Galen.

A few minutes later, Ralph Sylvester stepped through the doors of the shop, and immediately, I saw a smile cross over his face as he stood in front of the display Mart had put together. He lifted a copy of *The Green Book* and gently let the pages spin past his fingers. Then, he set it back down carefully, gazed at it another minute, and then picked up a copy of Isabel Wilkerson's *The Warmth of Other Suns* before heading to the armchair next to Mayhem and Taco and beginning to read.

I looked around the rest of the store – most of the chairs were full of people reading or talking with one another. The café was buzzing, and Mart's tasting line was impressive, even with the extra help she'd called in from the winery. As Marcus swung by after doing a quick pick-up of the store, I asked him to take over the register so I could step out and take a look at the fair and see how Cate and Lucas were doing.

When I walked out onto the sidewalk, I took a deep breath of warm spring air. It was gorgeous out here. The sun was sharing her perfect spring glow, making everything sparkle just a bit, and I figured the temperature was in the mid-sixties. I couldn't have ordered a better weather day. The sheriff had been right.

I gave Cate a wave as I stepped out into the street and looked back at the shop. She was busy telling people about her books, and I could see Lucas nearby doing the same. Several people had stacks of books in their hands, and the smile on Cate's face confirmed that she was happy to have made the decision to donate her books for the scholarship fund.

The middle of the road was full of people – many with cups of coffee from our café and the other restaurants – and I noticed a fair number of cinnamon rolls and the tell-tale remnants of icing on a few faces. Most of all, though, people looked happy . . . that kind of happy that comes when you are outside on the first warm day of spring, when you have the promise of a garden to plant and picnics to plan, when everything feels like it's opening up after the long, dark days of winter. Right then and there, I decided this would have to be an annual affair, and I thought how lovely it would be to schedule it the same time we did the Welcome to Spring event at the shop. Maybe call the whole thing The Welcome to Spring fair.

I was letting myself daydream about Stephen and Walter coming in to coordinate the event, maybe even construct a small stage for music at the end of the road, and seeing Galen as our media chair with Marcus managing the shop while I coordinated the readers and advertising. I could feel myself smiling as I realized that all my hard work over the past six months, that the utter change in my life since moving from San Francisco, had been worth it in every way.

I was content.

And then, I heard the shouting. It was coming from up the street, just beside Max Davies' shop. "You enabled her, you old coot." Max was angry. His voice was all screechy, and clearly, he wasn't worried about drawing negative attention because his voice could beat the band.

I hurried over, hoping to defuse the situation before the pleasant mood of this Sunday morning was disturbed. In front of Chez Cuisine, I found Max towering over Divina Stevensmith, who looked both furious and dangerous. Her hands were bunched at her sides, and she had drawn herself up to her full height so she could get closer to Max's face as he screamed at her. "You should have reined her in. She was your daughter," Max shouted.

"Don't you *dare* tell me how I should have raised my daughter, you ingrate. You have no idea!" All my interactions with Divina had given me a sense of her as a quiet, almost meek woman, but now, I was seeing her warrior side, and it was scary. I couldn't help but root for her though, after all the man was insulting her daughter, her dead daughter.

Their voices were getting louder as they continued to hurl insults at one another, and the crowd was gathering from up and down the street.

Oh man, this isn't good, I thought. The last thing we needed was to make this about murder when really it needed to be about the *life* of Deputy Williams.

Just when I thought I was going to have to step in and break it up, Elle Heron rushed over and stood between Max and Divina. I stepped closer with the idea of providing her back-up, but she didn't need me. In a low, growl of a voice, she said, "You two are making a scene. Max, go back inside. I'll come talk to you in a minute." She glared at him until he stomped his foot like a three-year-old and then went into his restaurant.

Elle then took Divina by the arm and led her away from the crowd, who had, thankfully, already started to disperse once the spectacle was over. I followed behind the two women, hoping I might be able to comfort Divina, get her a glass of water or something.

As I got closer behind them, I heard Elle say, "Seriously, you have the gall to cause a scene. You! You think no one knows, but I know. I know Divina."

The tiny, older woman looked at her and said, "If you know, then, you know I'm not someone to be trifled with. You best mind yourself, Elle. I will do what I need to do." Then Divina strode off back toward the co-op without so much as a backward glance.

I had no idea what I'd just heard, but I didn't think Divina had meant for me to hear that threat. Elle looked pretty shaken – but from anger or fear I couldn't tell. Still, I had to know what she knew, so I slid up behind her and laid a hand between her shoulder blades. She jumped and let out a little squeal.

"Oh, Elle, I'm so sorry," I said as I stepped around in front of her with my hands up. "I just heard what Divina said and wanted to be sure you were okay." I could see the tears pooled in her eyes, but I wasn't sure they were there because I startled her or because of what Divina had said. "What's going on?"

She looked around quickly and then took my elbow and led me to her shop and then into the back cooler where she kept the flowers. I shivered. I'd had a bad experience in a cooler once, and given the circumstances, I didn't love being in here with Elle, although it was looking less and less like she was actually a suspect.

"Divina can't know I was talking to you about this. It'll put you in danger."

"Wait, what?! Danger? Are you in danger? From Divina? What is—?"

She put a finger up to her lips. "I'll explain. Just can I get a minute to catch my breath?" She gave me a little smile as she sat down on a chair in the corner and started selecting stems of flowers from the five-gallon buckets at her feet. Her hands were shaking, but she selected each blossom with attention and then arranged it skillfully in her fingers. By the time she had a glorious pastel bouquet of pink roses, baby's breath, and hyacinth, her hands were steady again, and she looked up at me. "I think Divina Stevensmith murdered her daughter and Deputy Williams."

I looked around, saw an empty bucket, and turned it over as a seat. I needed to sit down. "Does she know that you suspect her?" I had about five thousand other questions, but I figured she'd get to the answers soon enough, now that she was talking.

"I imagine she does now. I shouldn't have intervened back there, at least not that way, but I didn't want her ruining this day. It's so beautiful, and you worked so hard." She looked up at me, and I could see the tears in her eyes again.

I reached over and took the bouquet from her and slipped it into a vase full of water on a small table beside her. Then I slid my bucket closer and held her hands. "Oh, Elle. So the articles Cate saw?"

She let out a raspy laugh. "I wondered if that's why you all had come back in that day. Yeah, I was doing a little investigating, following a hunch. That day you came to ask about the flowers, I'd seen Divina back behind your shop, poking around. I asked her if she'd lost something, and she said she'd dropped a pair of scissors. We looked for a while but didn't find them. It was only when I got back here that I thought to wonder why she'd had scissors near your shop. That got me thinking."

I shook my head. Divina had pulled the same thing on us the previous night. I told Elle that story, and we sat quietly for a while. "The articles were research then, but not about Lucia. About her mom."

"Right. I was trying to figure out why Divina would kill her own daughter, but I didn't see anything that made sense." She studied her fingernails. "Then, when Deputy Williams got killed, it suddenly felt really unsafe. I mean, if she could kill twice . . . " She looked up at me with shock.

"I know just what you mean." I leaned back on my bucket and stretched my back. "Okay, but now we need a cover story, something that makes sense of what you just said to Divina, something that will get you out of her cross-hairs."

Elle nodded. "Or at least be believable enough that other people will think that's what we're fighting about. I can't be sure, but something tells me that Divina just wants to keep her secret from going public. Maybe she doesn't care that I know?"

I shrugged. "Maybe. But maybe we can be sure, too." I stood up and paced around the cooler and then struck on something. "What if I went over there and told her you felt terrible about accusing her, that you thought she was trying to steal the attention away from Deputy Williams with her donation."

Elle looked skeptical. "Do you think she'll buy that?"

"Maybe. I mean I think I can convince her. She's so private and this donation is so out of the ordinary—" I stopped mid-sentence because I just realized something. "She feels guilty."

"What?" Elle asked.

"She donated her work of art because she feels guilty about killing Deputy Williams. I'm sure of it." I headed toward the cooler door. "That makes perfect sense."

Elle trailed after me. "It does, but we still don't know why she did it."

She was right. Motive still wasn't clear, but I imagined Sheriff Mason could make more sense of that. But first, I needed to be sure Elle was safe.

I gave her a quick hug, told her to come by the shop when she closed up for the night, and that we'd make a plan from there. Then, I headed to the co-op in the hopes that I'd find Divina in her studio.

Chapter Thirteen

The kid with the gauges in his ears was still on duty, and when I told him I was hoping to see Ms. Stevensmith, he didn't bat an eye and took me right back to her studio. "She doesn't usually like to be disturbed." He said it with casual ease, as if it didn't matter to him if artists needed privacy or not. Given the circumstances, neither did I.

I knocked lightly on the door and then tried the knob. It was open, so I stepped in and saw Divina with her scissors working at her counter. She glanced up and then went right back to work.

"You heard about the incident on the street?" she said quietly.

"I did. I actually heard the incident." I took a deep breath and dug deep for my best sincere voice. "Are you okay? You seemed pretty upset."

My acting must have worked because she put down her scissors and laid her hands on the waist-high counter in front of her and sighed. "That Max Davies pushes my buttons. Can't let anything go." She winced at her own words, but I couldn't very well ask why. "One review in that newspaper, and he was after Lucia all the time. My daughter was not a kind human being. I'm not denying that.

But his escargot is kind of chewy." She let out a breathy laugh, and I relaxed a little.

I said, "Yeah, he does seem kind of incensed about something from, what, a few years ago."

She looked up abruptly then. "Well, time doesn't heal all wounds, my dear. But this wound of Max's, it's pretty petty." She came around the desk, and I double-checked to be sure the scissors stayed behind. I was glad to see them on the counter. "Sit." She pointed to two club chairs covered in red fabric at the edge of the studio.

I made my way over, being sure to keep myself between the door and Divina, even though I felt kind of silly. She sure didn't come off like a cold-blooded killer, and right now, she just seemed sad.

"I just talked to Elle," I almost whispered.

Her eyes darted to mine and narrowed. "Oh? What does she have to say for herself?"

The energy in the room had changed just like that. It was suddenly colder, sharper in here. "She's sorry for accusing you of trying to steal the attention away from Deputy Williams. She really is."

Divina turned her head to look at me from the corner of her left eye. "Oh, right. She is? Well, that's good." I could hear the hesitation in her voice, as if she was waiting to hear more.

"I explained that you'd donated the piece and had wanted to stay out of the limelight as much as possible, that you'd even insisted on not being a part of the fair directly because you really wanted to keep the focus on Deputy Williams." Divina was nodding and looking at me. "I told her your donation wasn't about you at all, but about taking care of your community."

She smiled then. "Thank you, Harvey. That's exactly it. If anything, I'd like to have donated the work anonymously. Maybe I should have done that, but sometimes," she looked past me toward the door of the studio, "sometimes, we just need to put our names to things, claim our responsibility for them. You know?" She kicked her eyes back to me.

I felt like something was being said that wasn't being said, but I wasn't about to ask. "I do know. Absolutely. Anyway, I just wanted to come as an emissary for Elle, who feels so terrible that she was too ashamed to come talk to you herself. I hope you'll forgive her." I stood up.

Divina stood with me. "Of course. Some slights need to be overlooked."

I faked a laugh that I hoped sounded more real than it felt. "Like chewy escargot."

"Exactly." She held the door open for me as I left, and when I looked back, she was still watching me. I shivered.

Back at the shop, Cate and Lucas's sales were winding down as they tended the shoppers of the last few dozen books. I caught Cate's eye as I passed, pointed inside, and said, "When you can. No rush." She must have read something in my face because she handed the copy of *Black Book*, a collection of Robert Mapplethorpe's photography, back to Lucas and followed me inside.

As we passed the café, I waved to Mart, who left the wine table to follow us. I gave Daniel a quick wave, too, and asked Marcus to take over the register for a few minutes. Then, the four of us huddled in the back room while I told them about what Elle had found, what I suspected about the reason for the art donation, and my conviction that Divina Stevensmith was our murderer.

With the facts laid out like that, no one disagreed. "Nice work, Harvey," Daniel said, "but now, it's time to call the sheriff."

"Wait." I could hear the anxiety in my voice. It felt really important to me to figure this out. "We don't have a motive yet. And there's no physical evidence. Just possibilities." I wanted to tell the sheriff, but I also wanted to give him everything he needed. After all, he'd lost his deputy and friend to this woman's actions. If I could spare him the pain of further investigation . . . "Just give me until tomorrow. If we can't figure it out by then, I'll call."

Daniel held his phone out in front of him, his finger still poised to hit the sheriff's number in his contacts. But then Mart reached over and lowered his arm. "We'll work together to figure it out," she said, "and we won't leave Harvey alone for a minute."

I smiled my best "I've got this" smile for Daniel, even though I could feel the tension in my shoulders starting to creep up the back of my neck. I had no idea how to figure this out by tomorrow.

———

We headed back out onto the floor, and I went to relieve Marcus at the register and tell him to go take a break, enjoy the nice weather. "Oh, I'm waiting for my mom. She texted a few minutes ago, said she'd be here soon."

Then, as if on cue, this gorgeous black woman with thin braids twisted into a crown came through the door, and Marcus's face lit up. "That her?" I asked behind my own smile.

"Yep," he looked at me as he headed toward his mom. "Do you mind if I introduce you?"

"Mind? I'd be offended if you didn't." He laughed and then went and hugged his mother before bringing her over to the counter. "Mrs. Dawson, you have raised one fine son."

"Thank you, Ms. Beckett. I'm glad you can see that, too." She reached across the counter to shake my hand. "And thank you, too, for giving Marcus work, and in a bookstore, no less. You know this boy loves books?"

"Oh yes, ma'am, I do. If he's not skating or working, he's reading."

Mrs. Dawson beamed. "It's very nice to meet you, Ms. Beckett."

"Harvey, please."

"Harvey, then. Marcus, you keep on doing your thing. I'm going to browse."

I leaned over to Marcus. "You're due a break. Why don't you give your mom the grand tour?"

"You sure? It's been kind of busy."

"I've got it." I pointed behind Marcus toward where Daniel was getting Taco and Mayhem a bowl of water. "I have help if I need it."

Marcus caught up to his mom, who had made a stop at the wine table first thing. *My kind of woman*, I thought.

The rest of the afternoon went by in a blur of activity. Between customers, I tried to ponder what possible reason a woman could have for killing her own child, but I kept coming up empty. Nothing about the idea of Divina killing her daughter made much sense. I could see, however, why she might have killed Deputy Williams to cover up the first murder. If the deputy had come upon something incriminating – what that would be I hadn't yet figured out either – Divina might have acted just to "tie up loose ends" as they say on the TV dramas.

By the end of the day, I still had no solid motivation for why Divina would kill Lucia Stevensmith, and it looked more and more like I'd have to tell the sheriff everything I knew in the morning. But I still had a few hours, and I was determined to make the most of them.

At 4:45, I started our normal closing ritual. I walked around and told the remaining customers that we would be closing soon and asked them to bring their final purchases to the registers. I turned off the neon sign and asked Daniel to scout for misplaced books and reshelve them. I peeked in and saw that Rocky and Phoebe were beginning their clean-up, too, and when Rocky caught my eye, she whisper-shouted, "Best day yet." I grinned. I was happy for her. Our arrangement was that she got thirty percent of the take from the café as well as her hourly wage, and I hoped these big sale days were helping cover the costs of her next semester at school.

Marcus and his mom had spent the better part of the afternoon recommending books to customers, and the customers were thrilled. They were a power duo, passing book titles back and forth between them and delighting the customers with the depth of their knowledge.

At five o'clock, the last customer headed out, and I locked the door behind them. Ms. Dawson stopped by the register while Marcus helped Daniel with the reshelves. "I heard about Ms.

Stevensmith," Ms. Dawson said, a frown on her face. "That woman had done me no kindness, but I never wished her ill either. Sad what happened to her."

I nodded. "It is. I'm sorry about what she did to you, though, although I have to admit that it was reading about that story and then hearing about Marcus's, er, situation that led me to try and get him some work."

She tilted her head. "Really? Well, then I suppose something good came out of it all, didn't it?"

"I guess it did. Actually, I know it did, especially for me. Marcus is amazing, and I hope he'll stay on here full-time, maybe even think about stepping in as my assistant manager once my payroll numbers allow for that."

Ms. Dawson looked down, and I thought I saw her wipe a tear away. "I expect he'd like that. I know I would. This place," she gestured around the shop with an open hand, "is good. Real good."

I blushed. "Thank you. I have a question for you, too. I don't know if you have room in your schedule for this, but I was wondering if I could hire you to write a book review for us each week – any book you want as long as I can order it for the store. Just a few paragraphs about why someone might want to read it?" I paused and tried to read the baffled expression on her face. "What do you think?

"You want to hire me to read books and write about them."

"Well, yes. I mean I can't pay much, surely not what you're worth—"

"Yes. I'd love to. You don't even have to pay me." She was bouncing on the balls of her feet. "Maybe Marcus and I can write some together sometime?"

"I love that idea, but I'm going to pay you. We all have to eat."

Marcus strolled over and looked from his mom to me. "What's going on?"

"I'll tell you about it over dinner. Tacos are on me." She pointed out the window toward Lu's truck.

I laughed. "See you at home later, Marcus?" I glanced at his mother really quickly, but clearly he had told her he was staying with Mart and me because she didn't bat an eye. "Tomorrow, when you come in, we'll talk about your full-time schedule, if that suits."

He looked at me with a wide smile. "That suits, Ms. B. See you later."

As they passed under the ringing bell, Mart came over, a box full of wine bottles under her arm. "That was kind of you, Harvey. I'll run the numbers tonight for you, see what kind of salary you can offer your new assistant manager."

I shrugged and smiled. "I could use the help."

"Yes, you could, and you can't help yourself. You love being kind to people. It's one of the things I love about you."

I started to hug her but stopped short. "Oh, Mart, but this doesn't mean I'm not going to start paying rent—"

"Gracious, Harvey Beckett. Of course, you're going to pay rent. I would never doubt that for a minute. I expect the last two weeks of income have you set up well for the rest of the month. Budgets, we'll work on budgets for both of us this week."

I gave her that hug now. "Okay, see you at home in a bit?"

"Yep, just going to drop off my trusty assistant," she gestured with her head at the young woman by the door, "and return these last bottles of wine to the winery – we sold all but five. BIG weekend for us. Then, I'll be back. Cereal for dinner?"

"Perfect. See you there."

I was just finishing the register count and putting together the bank deposit when Cate and Lucas knocked on the glass. I let them in and then looked outside. "You guys. You didn't have to put everything away. I was headed out to do that. You did so much already."

Cate wrapped her arms around my waist and squeezed. "Harvey, do you really think we did more than you did today? You put together this whole event and," she leaned over to whisper, "figured out who the murderer is. I think we can manage to fold up some tables."

I blushed, but then peeked out the window again. "Wait, where are all the books?"

Lucas clapped his hands and then rubbed them together. "We

sold all but about two dozen, and Mrs. Murphy, the librarian, came by and picked up the rest."

"Yep! She said they'll use some of them in their collection and the rest they'll let the kids in the summer program cut up for art projects." Cate laughed.

My hand flew to my mouth. "Oh no, Cate, your books."

"Are you kidding me? Kids making art out of copies of art — that's almost better than the $4,283 we raised for the scholarship fund."

I dropped into the arm chair next to the Eastern Shore history shelf. "Whoa. That's a lot of money."

"Yep. Most of it came from book sales, but a few people gave a little extra." Lucas pulled a wad of cash out of his pocket and showed it to me, careful to keep his body between the window and the money. "I'll take it to the sheriff's department in the morning, but for now, I think we're headed home . . . unless you need us to help with anything?"

"Like figuring out a motive," Cate piped in.

I sighed. "Oh, thanks, guys, but honestly, at this point, I'm too tired. I really wanted to figure this out for the sheriff, save him the work, but I'm at a loss. I'll just call him in the morning."

Cate hugged me again. "Sounds wise, Harvey. Sounds very wise. Get on home and get some rest."

I locked the door behind them and finished my count. I had just returned to the chair by the fiction section — a seat that was quickly becoming my favorite — when I heard another knock at the door. "I'll get it. You rest," Daniel said to me as he stepped around the shelf to look toward the front of the store. "It's Elle. I'll take the dogs for a walk while you two talk for a few minutes, see if you can piece anything together."

"Okay, sounds good. But come back quickly will you? I'm tuckered and ready to go home."

He leaned down and kissed my cheek before heading to let Elle in. I heard the tinkle of the bell and the jingle of the dogs' tags as he slipped out.

Elle looked more composed than she had earlier, and I was glad to see it. I stood up and gestured to the comfy chair, but she pulled over the wingback from the history section and plopped into it.

"Long day, huh?" I asked as I settled back into my seat, tucking my feet under me.

"So long . . . it was great in terms of business. I sold out of everything except for a few bunches of Dusty Miller that no one but a florist really knows how to use." She let out a long sigh. "But in terms of Divina, I don't even know what to do."

I let out my own matching exhale and nodded.

"How did she seem with your explanation about what I meant about her knowing what she did?"

I thought back over that conversation, somehow less convinced than I had been that I'd gotten through to her. I didn't think it would help Elle to know that though, so I said, "I think she heard me, probably believed me, too. When I left her, she sounded like she was going to let things go."

Elle let her head fall back. "Okay, good. At least she doesn't know we're on to her." Her head snapped forward. "But what do we do now?"

"We tell the sheriff. First thing tomorrow, you and I go in and tell him what we know, and we let him take it from there." I felt disappointed, but also relieved with that decision. I still wanted to spare him the work – and I really wanted to satisfy my own curiosity about Divina's motive – but none of that justified letting a murderer be free any longer.

"Sounds like a good plan." She stood up. "I forgot to ask. Things go okay here?"

I stood alongside her and heard the doorbell ring as Daniel came back. "They did. We raised a lot of money for the scholarship fund, and I think the shop did really well, too."

I started to walk her to the door, but as we stepped around the local history shelf, we met the muzzle of a shotgun. Behind it, Divina Stevensmith was steady as an ocean breeze. "I think we have something to discuss, ladies."

I tried to step toward the front of the store, but Divina swung her shotgun and herded me back before putting herself between me and the front door. Then, she started walking forward as Elle and I slowly stepped backward, trying not to trip over dog beds or bump into bookshelves. The whole time I was hoping that Divina had locked the front door so that Daniel wouldn't come in and get himself shot while I also tried to figure out how to call for help.

"We're just going to have a conversation, be sure we're clear on some things." As soon as we reached the bathroom doors, Divina stopped. She pointed the gun right into Elle's face and said, "You just had to be nosy." Then, she swung the barrel until it grazed my nose, "And you just had to be kind. If you'd both minded your own business, this would all be behind us. Now, I have to sully Berkeley's place again."

My brain wasn't really firing correctly, but I did manage to say, "Divina, I don't know what you're talking about."

She moved the barrel down and shoved it into my sternum. "Stop it. Don't play dumb. It doesn't suit you. You know I killed Lucia and Deputy Williams, God rest her soul. Poor woman. If she hadn't come patrolling that night . . ."

I still was having trouble forming complete thoughts, but something clicked, and I could picture Divina there at the back of the shop with a sage smudging stick as Deputy Williams came around the building.

"I might have been able to get her to leave if I'd just told her the truth, but I couldn't. And then she started asking a lot of questions . . . about Lucia and the umbrella. I didn't know she knew about the umbrella." She looked like she might cry for a split second, but then, a wash of determination came over her face. "I did what I had to do. Berkeley's place had to be cleansed, and I couldn't let her take me away before I finished."

Elle grabbed my hand, and I tried to focus on her touch so that it would let my brain work behind the scenes of my fear. "So you were smudging the place Berkeley died? The place those hateful people killed him, trying to purify his shop." I wasn't sure I knew what I was talking about, but I must have been close because Divina's face crumpled.

"This place was a safe haven. It was pure, untainted." She took a shuddering breath, and then her voice was cold as steel, "but those monsters, they stole Berkeley and they ruined this building."

"Oh, Divina, that's awful." I didn't have to work hard to feign sympathy. I could see her there as a young woman, hiding in the bushes while her husband was murdered. "But Divina, why didn't you seek justice then? Why not go to the police with what you knew?"

Her eyes locked on mine. "You think I didn't try that. Of course I tried that, but our marriage was illegal . . . so no one had to listen to me as his wife." Her voice broke then. "Besides, one of the men who killed Berkeley . . ." Her jaw was so tight I thought she might break her teeth.

"One of them was a police officer," Elle's voice was very quiet.

Divina nodded, and I felt a tug to go hug her. The shotgun shut down that impulse though.

"I knew there would never be justice. I just tried to tamp it down, let it go like people said to do. And I thought I had . . . "

I willed myself to make the connection, to figure out what all this had to do with the fact that she had murdered her daughter, but I couldn't tie it together.

Elle got it, though. "Then, your daughter wrote those horrible things about Harriet Tubman, another hero who provided safe haven for travelers."

Elle was far better than me under pressure. She'd put it together. All of Divina's suppressed trauma and rage had come boiling out when she'd seen her daughter's hateful comments about the hero who had helped found the Underground Railroad.

"I couldn't believe any child of mine would be so ignorant." She shook her head violently. "I tried to talk to her, explain, tell her about Berkeley, but she was so arrogant. She just kept waving around those sheets of horrid orange paper that she used for her notes, telling me that she was just offering an 'alternative perspective.'"

I slipped my hand around the wall, easing it upward ever so slowly.

"Before I knew it, the umbrella was in my hand, and—"

"You didn't mean to kill her," Elle said, giving my hand a squeeze.

Divina's eyes were blazing. "Of course, I didn't. The umbrella was heavier than I thought . . . and I was so angry."

I kept inching my fingers upward and feeling for the alarm keypad.

"Before I could help her, she came in here, and I couldn't force myself to follow her. I thought she'd be okay, wake up the next day with a nasty headache but be okay."

Elle started to step forward with her right hand out, but Divina whipped the shotgun up again. I froze, my finger just at the bottom of the keypad.

"Now, though, I need to finish what I started. Get things tidied up." She looked around the store. "You've done a good job here, Harvey— Wait! What are you doing? Don't move a muscle."

She stalked over to me and grabbed my left arm. Then, she sighed. "Into the storeroom. Both of you."

I wasn't willing to take my eyes off Divina, and apparently Elle had the same thought because we inched our way backward again. I stepped back through the doorway first, and then Elle followed after me. Divina closed the door behind her and then leaned back against it, her breathing heavy.

I was desperate. I needed to keep her talking. "You know this is where Lucia died. I know you know that. And Deputy Williams died just behind here. You're back there smudging the bathroom door, smudging the bathroom over at the courthouse where you hid until Berkeley's murderers left. There's no amount of sage that is going to undo that much bloodshed and sorrow, Divina." I was saying anything to change her mind while I hoped that Elle had an idea of how to get out of here.

Divina sighed. "I know. But my art is the way I make good on the awful things I've done."

"You mean by donating it to the scholarship fund to cover up your guilty conscience?" Elle asked. Apparently, Elle and I weren't on the same wavelength about how to deal with the homicidal woman. I wanted to placate her, dissuade her. Elle was apparently going for antagonism.

"Oh, I didn't donate that painting because I felt guilty – at least not entirely. Nope, that was about telling the story of that night. I expect neither of you noticed, but there's a black man chasing down two men on horses with a shotgun in that piece. It's subtle, almost a secret, just like Berkeley's murder has been kept secret all these years."

I tried to remember the details of the art piece from when I'd looked at it earlier, but I couldn't recall anything that resembled a person chasing two men on horseback. It had looked like an abstract collage with hints of the town buildings to me. But then, I didn't know art. Maybe that story was there . . . or maybe Divina was more mentally unwell than we knew and just thought it was.

"My art is my work of justice. And I'm not done yet. So I'm afraid you will have to be." She lowered the shotgun while she scanned the room. "I don't want to ruin your inventory. You've done such a nice job of creating this store. I know Berkeley would love it, and that display at the front, the one with *The Green Book*, that's beautiful. Now, we need a place—"

Just then, the door burst open, and Mayhem charged the petite woman just as I jumped forward to grab her gun. A shot went off, and I spun around in some sort of *Matrix*-inspired attempt to dodge a bullet I suppose.

The spray of shot blasted into a stack of books just as Daniel tackled Divina and I wrested the gun from her hands. Mayhem stood growling over her, and Taco waddled over to check on Elle.

A few seconds later, Sheriff Mason ran into the room, gun raised, but when he saw that Daniel had Divina firmly by the wrists, he holstered his weapon and put the artist in handcuffs.

Elle and I ran to each other and hugged, tears streaming down our faces. Then, we turned to face Divina, only to be met with a blank stare, as if she couldn't even see us.

As the sheriff escorted Divina out, he turned to us. "I'll need your statements, ladies, but why don't I come to your place and get them, Harvey? Daniel, you can get them home?"

"Absolutely." He came to me then and wrapped me in a deep hug before pulling Elle to him, too.

When we got to my house, Mart met us at the door with blankets and mugs of hot chocolate spiked with what I suspected was whiskey. Daniel had apparently texted her about what happened as we walked over. I had insisted on walking, and Elle had agreed. We both needed the cool night air to calm our heart rates.

Mart installed both Elle and me on the sofa, and Aslan came to settle right between us. Daniel called Cate and Lucas and texted Marcus and Rocky. Soon everyone, including Woody Isherwood, was in our living room with looks of concern written deep on their faces. Not a single one of our friends asked us about what had happened, but they kept checking to be sure we were warm enough, asking if we needed more hot cocoa – or straight shots of whiskey if Woody was doing the asking – and getting us snacks every few minutes.

By the time the sheriff arrived, I was calmer and so exhausted that I wondered if I might drift off there right in the midst of everybody. When Mason said he needed to take our statements, everyone but Elle and me headed to the kitchen within earshot, but far enough away to give us space.

We told the sheriff what happened, what had led us to believe that Divina was the murderer and what she'd confessed to us. "You didn't happen to record all that, did you?" he said with a wry grin.

"Alas, no, I was a little more worried about getting shot than I was about getting my phone out." I tried to laugh, but the sound caught in my throat.

Elle smiled. "I actually thought about it, but since I can barely turn on the flashlight on my phone, I figured I couldn't be stealthy enough to actually record anything. With my luck, I'd probably start playing Queen's "We Are The Champions" instead."

I giggled at the image of Freddy Mercury's voice filling up the bookshop, and then I started to laugh for real. Soon, I was doubled over and breathless with laughter. . . and then I was sobbing. The sheriff motioned for Daniel to come in, and I felt a warm arm pull me close as I let myself cry.

After I caught my breath, Sheriff Mason said, "I was mostly kidding about the recording. Divina confessed to everything in the car, told me pretty much the same thing you did. Even mentioned dropping the knife and going back to find it. That's what she was doing the night we caught her back there."

I turned to Elle. "You put things together quickly – how did you know about the Tubman connection?"

"I don't know. It just sort of came together in my head, and I said it before I had a chance to think. Looking back, it all seems sort of obvious."

"It always does," the sheriff said. "It's too bad justice couldn't have been served back then. Maybe we wouldn't have had to serve it now." He stood up and headed for the door, and I couldn't help but wondering how he was doing. Now didn't seem the time to ask, though.

"So that's it. Nothing else," I said.

"Nope, nothing else. Daniel had already given me the heads up about Divina earlier today, so I was planning on picking her up for questioning tomorrow. You two just saved me the trouble."

I gave Daniel a quick glance. He shrugged and gave me a sad smile.

Somehow, I didn't think that our investigation was exactly making less work for the sheriff, but I was glad the murderer was off the streets. Mason waved as he headed toward his car.

Lucas and Cate gave me a hug and offered to give Elle a lift home, and Woody headed out at the same time. Mart and Marcus offered to do clean-up, so Daniel and I drifted back to the couch.

"You couldn't wait until tomorrow, huh?" I wanted to be angry with him, but I just couldn't.

"No, I couldn't. I was too worried. And I don't know you well, but I know you well enough to know you weren't going to let this go." His face fell. "I should have been there tonight, though. Harvey, I'm so sorry. I thought you were safe with Elle there."

I scooted closer to him, folding my legs and leaning over to grab his shoulders. "Me, too. I had really hoped Divina had bought my story about Elle. But I guess she didn't . . . we did make it a little too easy for her, though, both of us being together. Two birds with one—"

"Nope, too soon. No killing metaphors, please."

I turned and let myself lean against him, and he pulled me close and tucked a blanket around my legs.

Chapter Fourteen

By the next morning, the entire day before felt like a dream – one that had gone from delightful to nightmare. I had mostly relegated Divina's actions to the past, vowing to not forget them or to ignore them, but to not dwell in the darkness either.

Mart took a day off from the winery – a well-earned one since she'd signed up a record number of folks for their subscription offering during the festival the day before – and came in to help me run the shop. Marcus was right on time as usual, and Rocky came in with a plate full of muffins. "Mama says muffins are for recovery, so this is for you." She handed me a white paper bag that was hand-decorated with beautiful drawings of hyacinths. Inside was a single muffin in a bright blue paper and a note, "You are strong, Harvey Beckett. Never forget that. – Love, Mama Phoebe."

I didn't even wait for the tears to stop before I took a bite right out of the top of that muffin – banana nut with more walnuts in it than I'd ever had in a muffin before. I could taste the vanilla, and the caramelized sugar on top crunched on my teeth. But those walnuts, "Oh woman, you tell your mama that she knows how to help a woman recover." Rocky laughed and headed to the shop.

The sheriff came by later to tell me that Divina had been arraigned first thing. She was foregoing a trial because, in her words, "I want to spare the town any more drama." She'd be sentenced later in the week.

"Now, maybe you can stick to bookselling and leave the police work to me," he said as he headed out the door to tell Elle the news about Divina's case.

"Maybe." I said, never one to make promises I couldn't keep.

Daniel came by at lunch with tacos from Lu's truck, and we sat at a table in the café with cups of fresh limeade that Rocky had decided to add to her menu. The drink tasted amazing, but I couldn't bring myself to eat much.

"Lu Mason is going to come in here and demand an explanation if you don't eat that carnitas, Ms. Beckett." Daniel's voice was teasing, but there was concern in his eyes.

I looked up at him. "It's not the taco. I just keep thinking about Berkeley Hudson and that night. He did so much for so many people, and no one, even in his town, knows his story."

Daniel nodded. "It is sad."

The next week went by without event. Galen came by on Thursday with Mack, the most adorable senior bulldog I'd ever seen. He, Mayhem, and Taco, who had started spending days at the shop since he was a bit, um, under foot in the garage, became fast friends and all shared one giant bed that I'd added back by the self-help section.

Elle brought flowers to the shop every morning, and we became fast friends. Near death will do that to you. Even Max Davies seemed to take a shine to the shop and stopped by from time to time to offer his expert wisdom on our cookbook selection.

Ms. Dawson wrote her first column for our weekly newsletter and recommended Ta-Nehisi Coates' *The Water Dancer*. Her review was astute and honest, giving caution for our readers with ancestors who had been enslaved, but also suggesting the great power of the book for all readers. We got several requests for the book almost immediately, and I was delighted to send a check by way of Marcus that first week.

Business stayed brisk, brisk enough that I was able to hire Woody to make a bench for in front of the shop window so that people could relax outside in the warmer weather. Cate helped me expand the art book section and managed to restrain herself and only order two books for herself. "My husband will definitely divorce me if I start hoarding books again," she said. Lucas held true to his word and helped me develop a sizable maritime section with historical books, books on boats, and even a nice collection of fiction with nautical themes.

Marcus continued to prove himself invaluable, and I was on track to bring him on as assistant manager by the end of the spring. He finished *Possession* in half the time it had taken me and declared it "good but a little too purposefully obtuse," which was an assessment I could not argue with. He moved into Daniel's apartment within a few weeks and loved it, and I enjoyed watching him skate to work every morning and home every night with a little more lightness in his frame.

And Daniel, well, he walked me home every night. Some of those nights – mostly the ones when Mart was out of town – he stayed late, but we still hadn't had our first sleepover. That would come, I knew, but for now, we were taking it slow. The way I liked it best.

One day in mid-April, Ralph Sylvester stopped in. I hadn't seen him since the day of the street fair, but I'd thought of him often, wondering if he'd come by after he heard about what happened with Divina. When he showed up, I realized I had been nervous, worried that he was angry with me for having his friend's wife arrested. But as soon as I saw his smile, I knew he harbored no such resentment. He was – unlike some of us – a man who worked through his pain and came out the other side stronger.

"Harvey, it's so good to see you," he said as he reached out a hand and took mine. "I'm sorry I've been away for so long. I didn't want to come back until I had something for you." From behind his back, he pulled a square about the size of a trade paperback and all wrapped in tissue paper. "I hope I'm not being presumptuous in giving it to you."

I furrowed my brow and then took the package from his hand. "Well, thank you." I peeled back the paper, read the words, and felt the tears begin.

In this location, Berkeley Hudson ran The Hudson Station from 1928–1958. This building and Hudson's home, with his wife Divina, were safe havens for black people from all over the South. This building is memorialized in *The Green Book* and will forever be a place of safety for people who need respite and rejuvenation, be that through fuel or word.

"Oh, Mr. Sylvester, thank you!" I took a deep breath to keep from sobbing. "I don't know what to say."

"Well, maybe you'll hang it up."

I looked at him with shock. "No maybe about it. I'm hanging it now. Hold on." I spun around as if a masonry drill was going to fall from the ceiling.

"Maybe this will help." Woody came through the door, drill in hand. "Ralph stopped by to ask if he could borrow it." He put out a hand and took the plaque. "But I'd be honored if you'd let me hang it."

I nodded, tears stealing my voice again. I pointed to a spot at eye level just to the right of the front door. "I want everyone to see it."

Mr. Sylvester nodded. "I like that idea."

A few moments later, the bronze plaque hung where every single person who left this building would notice it and be reminded. It was the perfect, final touch for my store.

For a few weeks, I continued to avoid the storeroom – too many hard memories there. When I absolutely had to go in, I'd rush to whatever I needed and rush back out, ignoring everything else. But eventually, I knew I had to deal with the aftermath of Divina's visit. The police had gathered all the evidence they needed weeks earlier, but it was up to me to deal with the damaged inventory.

I took a deep breath and headed for the box the shotgun blast had blown open. Fragments of paper were scattered all around, reminding me of Lucia Stevensmith's orange notepaper, and I dreaded not only the reliving of the memory but the travail of dealing with the damaged books. As I opened the lid, pellets tinkled out on the ground, I thought I might cry again . . . but then, I caught a glimpse of the cover on the top book. *Riding Shotgun* by Rita Mae Brown. How fitting, I thought, and started to laugh.

And keep turning the page for a free preview of Entitled to Kill, book 2 in the St Marin's series.

Mother-daughter bonding time shouldn't involve running from a big tractor.

When Harvey Beckett stumbles upon the body of the community's most reviled dairy farmer, she, her friends, and her parents are launched into an investigation that reveals a family secret that wasn't really that secret after all.

Turn the page for a free preview…

Entitled to Kill: Chapter One

If asked to name my favorite season, I'd immediately say fall. But I also have a deep affection for the first really warm days of spring, the ones when all the flowers are bursting forth, when tulips bejewel front yards and the cherry trees begin to flower the air with their petals.

It was late April in St. Marin's, and spring was fully here. My bookstore had been open an entire month, and it was actually turning a profit. A small profit, but a profit nonetheless. I'd even begun paying part of the mortgage on our house. Mart, my best friend and roommate, had tried to convince me to wait until at least July before I began to contribute, but I had insisted. I wasn't paying anywhere near half, but writing that first check had felt gratifying, like I'd begun to make it as a business owner.

My bookstore, All Booked Up, had been my dream for as long as I could remember. Even as a child, I'd imagined myself surrounded by books, a dog at my feet, reading all day. The business end of things came later, but mostly, I was living the dream, as they say. Okay, I didn't do as much reading as I might like, but I did have the "dog at my feet and surrounded by books" part down.

Mayhem, my trusty Black Mouth Cur sidekick, had settled right in as the shop pup, and she enjoyed welcoming the neighborhood canines – and brave felines – over for a visit, too. I had almost as many dog beds as I did armchairs in the shop, and some days, every comfy seat – both elevated and floor-level – was occupied with someone enjoying a read or a nap. And it wasn't always the dogs that were napping.

I loved that people had already begun to feel comfortable enough in the store to just come, pick up a book, and read an hour away. I didn't want to own the kind of store where people felt like they had to come in, get their books, and leave. When someone returned time and again to read the same book, I found that endearing. Not all of us have the funds to buy books, and while I was a huge patron of the local library, I fully appreciated that some-times the best place to read was where noise was allowed and the air smelled like coffee.

Our bookstore's little café filled up what had once been the garage bay when this was a gas station. It was small and quaint, and it served the best latte this side of Annapolis. Rocky was the manager of that part of the store, and her share of the profits was helping fund her BA down at Salisbury University. Sometimes her mom, Phoebe, came in and helped out for big events, and that woman made cinnamon rolls so good they felt like a Hallmark movie Christmas morning.

I was counting on the draw of her rolls on this Saturday morning because we were having our first author event that night, and I needed to get a buzz going in town. I'd done all the usual marketing – on- and off-line – but my guest author was local, and I knew we needed the small-town crowd to make this event successful.

David Healey wrote military thrillers and mysteries set here on the Eastern Shore of Maryland, and he had a loyal readership. I just didn't know how many of those readers lived close enough by to come to the shop for his evening reading, but I was hoping that the fact that he was from Chesapeake City might bring out a banner crowd.

We'd marketed David's reading as part of a "Welcome to Spring" weekend with the hopes that people would spend at least the day, maybe even Saturday and Sunday, in St. Marin's. The hardware store had gotten in a new supply of kitschy, crab-themed T-shirts, and the art co-op had arranged a special exhibition of local artists. I had coordinated the event with the maritime museum's annual boat-skills exhibition, and Elle Heron had created a special "Get Your Garden In Right" workshop for the afternoon. We even had a special "Eastern Shore Prix Fixe" menu set up at Chez Cuisine, a few doors down. People could come and enjoy the events of the day. The cinnamon rolls would just get the day started right.

Even if the guests didn't flock to our doors in droves, I knew I really needed a big warm concoction of flour, yeast, cinnamon, and cream cheese icing. That and Rocky's biggest latte should get me past my nerves. A lot of people were counting on this day to bolster their sales until the full-on tourist season of summer began in our waterside town, and I could feel the weight of their expectations as I unlocked the front door.

The bell that had hung over the front door of the shop since it was a gas station tinkled as I opened it, and I smiled. I would never tire of that sound.

I was swinging the door shut behind me when I felt it thud against something. I turned back to see a Basset Hound head wedged between the door and the frame. "Oh, Taco. I'm so sorry." I swung the door open. "I didn't see you there."

The Basset charged right ahead, my insulting behavior forgotten, as he saw Mayhem just ahead of me on her leash. I did my best jump rope maneuvers over the quickly tangling leashes and looked up to see Taco's owner, Daniel, smiling at me.

I felt a warm flush go up my neck and wondered if I'd ever see this man I'd been dating and not have my face turn red. We'd been a couple – that's what Mart said people in town were calling us – ever since the shop opened, but I still got all nervous when I first saw his dark hair, fair skin, and brown eyes. I found him so handsome, and he was everything my ex-husband hadn't been – reliable, attentive, and willing to take care of me even though he knew I didn't need him to do that.

Still, I was forty-four years old and totally unclear on what to call him. Was he my boyfriend? Did middle-aged women have boyfriends? *Lover* just sounded way too racy for our perfectly slow relationship, and *partner* was far too much. *Friend* didn't work either because that sounded like what my grandmother would have said, "Daniel is Harvey's 'special friend.'" I defaulted to "Daniel" instead. That worked most of the time, although a couple of times I had slipped and said, "My Daniel" as if he was a stuffed animal or I was differentiating him from another Daniel, like that guy in the lion's den I'd learned about in childhood Sunday School classes.

I liked the guy, though. A lot, even if I didn't know what to call him. And Mayhem felt much the same about his pup, Taco. I didn't really buy into the whole dog love affairs craze myself, but these two were at the least best pals.

Already, they'd sniffed out the best bed for the day – the one in the front window's sunbeam beside the display of books on shipwrecks – and were lying butt to butt and snoring. The dog's life was something.

As Daniel and I made our way to the front counter, he gave me a quick kiss on the cheek. "So aside from trying to decapitate my dog, how has your day been so far?"

"Well, I have to say it just got a whole lot better." I had never been a flirtatious person before, but this man, for some reason he brought it out in me.

A blush flew into his cheeks, too, and we stood grinning at one another until the sound of a throat clearing broke our gaze. Rocky was standing in front of the counter across from us with a grin a mile wide on her face. "Sorry. I thought you'd heard me come in."

I looked toward the front door. I *hadn't* heard the bell ring. "No, I'm sorry. How are you? How's studying for finals going?"

She let out a long, slow sigh. "It's going." She pulled her thick handful of tiny braids into a hair tie and then dropped a heavy tote bag onto the counter. "I mean, I love my classes, but I had a very high opinion of my reading speed and retention ability when I signed up for three English and two history classes. Finals are in two weeks, and I have five books to read and three papers to write to even get to the finals."

"Whew, that's a lot. What are your professors thinking?" I remembered my college days when I was an English and History double major just like Rocky. One semester, I'd had to buy sixty-seven books. Sixty-seven. I loved books, but that was ridiculous.

"They're thinking that their class is the most important one. They've all forgotten what it's like to have five classes and a job."

Daniel laughed. "That, right there, ladies, is why I didn't finish college. Too much reading."

I never in my life thought I'd date a man who didn't read, but here I was, full on in the throes of like – I wasn't ready for the other L word yet – with a man who took it as a point of pride that the last full book he read was the copy of *Tom and Jerry Meet Little Quack* that his mom found in a box of his first-grade mementos.

It wasn't that Daniel didn't appreciate knowledge or books, and it certainly wasn't that he wasn't smart – the man could disassemble and then reassemble a car engine in less than two hours, a feat I understood to be impressive, even though my knowledge of cars stopped at the fact that Brits called the trunk of the car the "boot." No, Daniel was plenty smart. He just couldn't sit still long enough to read. His body needed to be moving. Even when we watched TV – lately, we'd been binge-watching a show I'd loved a few years back, *The 4400* – he put together model cars. He just couldn't be completely still, and school required a lot of stillness.

I didn't mind the car-building stuff, though, because he'd inspired me to make use of my downtime, too. I'd picked back up my cross-stitch hobby after years of neglect. And like most things in my life, I didn't start slow. I bought a kit of a cat in a bookshop. It was beautiful – all bright colors and a black and white cat with a few extra pounds that reminded me of my own girl, Aslan. But it was also immense – maybe 18 x 24 on small-count fabric – and every square called for a stitch. At this rate, I'd finish it in when I was seventy. Still, it was relaxing because it required my attention and let my mind slow down. It was the only way I'd found, so far, to stop thinking about the shop. Well, cross-stitch and kissing Daniel.

Rocky hefted her heavy bag onto her shoulder and headed to the café while Daniel carried the platter of her mom's cinnamon rolls behind her. I'd slipped one out from under the plastic and sat savoring the doughy goodness while I checked emails.

Everything seemed to be in order for the day. David Healey had written to say he'd be in town by noon and wondered if I could grab lunch to talk about the night's event. I shot back a quick response with my cell number and told him to text me when he arrived. Then, I answered enough queries about parking and general activities in town that by the time we opened at ten, I felt confident we were going to have a great day.

About ten thirty, Mart arrived with Cate, our friend who ran the art coop. They'd been out on the bay kayaking, trying to capture photos of some watermen at work for Cate's new portrait series. Mart was on hand to run the register in case things got busy, and Cate was going to lead a plein air painting group that was meeting here at eleven. Both of them were rosy cheeked and equally pleasant tempered. Part of me wished I'd been able to go, but most of me was quite content to have spent the morning answering questions about books, making notes about titles we needed to order back in, and enjoying Phoebe's cinnamon roll. Sure, I missed out on some things by running the shop, but what I got to do, well, it more than made up for it.

"Looks like you've got things well in hand," Mart said.

"Now, let's not be too hasty, Martha." Cate put on a serious face as she brushed her short black hair out of her eyes. "The true test is whether she—"

I reached below the counter and pulled out two saucers, each adorned with a cinnamon roll.

Cate laughed. "Yep, all in hand here."

When I'd met Cate a few weeks ago, I hadn't realized that Mart and I really needed a third to make our friendship even more amazing, but it turns out that the third we were missing was a short, Korean-American photographer whose husband cooked really, really well.

Mart and I had been friends for years back in San Francisco, and when I'd decided to return home to Maryland last fall, she'd decided to come along. She, by far, looked the youngest of all of us with her fair skin that showed nary a wrinkle and her thick, brown hair that she wore in soft waves or in a ponytail that, somehow, managed to look amazing. My curly, quickly-graying short hair did not always fare so well in the wind and moisture of a waterside town, and I took to rolled bandanas on days when I didn't want to look like Lyle Lovett or to spend an hour with a flat iron. (I never wanted to spend an hour with a flat-iron.) Also, I had wrinkles in my pale, pinkish skin, including a furrow between my eyes that would never smooth out again.

Many women never get to have one good friend in the world, and I was lucky enough to have two. In both literal and figurative ways, they had each saved my life, and I was so glad we got to see each other every day, even if they teased me no end about having a boyfriend. They always insisted on saying it *boooyyyfriend*, like we were eleven. Still, I adored them.

My friends tucked into their cinnamon rolls with all the genteelness of vultures on roadkill, and I couldn't help but smile. No pinkies in the air here. I'm pretty sure I even caught Mart licking the plate when I turned around to get more bags to put under the counter.

Snacks done and coffee procured from Rocky, they got to work, and I began my usual circuit around the store, just to be sure things were tidy, but not pristine. Something about a little bit of disheveled order felt home-like, comfortable.

I was just rounding the corner of the religion section when I spied a familiar pair of Jordans propped on a shelf next to a wing-back chair. I slipped behind the seat and peeked over the top to get a look at the title of the book the person was reading. "*The Water Dancer*. I hear that's really good."

Marcus Dawson slowly lowered his book, pulled his brown legs down as I stepped around in front of him, and smiled up at me. "It's amazing," he said, "but no spoilers. You have to read it yourself."

"Will do." I kicked his shin playfully. "You know, you don't have to be here when you're not working."

He shrugs. "What can I say? When you find a good thing . . ."

Marcus had started working here almost a month ago, and he was amazing at his job – thoughtful with his recommendations and voracious in his reading. At first, I'd hired him to help him out, but it turned out that he was a major draw for returning customers who found his book suggestions to be so fitting for them that they came in just to talk to him about the previous recommendation and pick up a new one.

Now, he had a regular column in our weekly newsletter, where he did book matchmaking with customers who filled out a short survey as they stopped by. I'd gotten the idea from one of my favorite podcasts, *What Should I Read Next?*, and people were loving it. Our box of completed surveys was so full that we were talking about doing Instagram videos to accommodate more customer requests. I had definitely gotten the better end of the deal when I'd hired Marcus.

On Monday, he would begin his first shift as assistant manager. I noticed he'd had his hair cut into a shorter version of his typical box fade and wondered again if all the things from my teenage years were coming back: high-waisted jeans, fanny packs, and shoulder pads. It made me shiver. Marcus's hair though, I loved. I couldn't help but think of Kid 'n Play when I saw him, but I wouldn't make the mistake of mentioning them again since Marcus had looked at me like I was approximately eight hundred years old the one time I'd brought them up.

I'd given him the weekend off so that he could relax, spend time with his mom, and maybe even do something fun in Annapolis or Baltimore, but I wasn't all that surprised to see him in the store. He really did seem to love St. Marin's and my bookshop, and I knew that living in his apartment above Daniel's garage was probably kind of lonely, especially when Daniel wasn't at work. Plus, I just liked him and liked having him around.

"Well, happy reading. But no working today. Not even Insta photos. It's your day off. I don't want to pay you, but I'll be forced to if you work, you hear me?" I gave his leg another nudge and headed off to help Daniel, who was bringing up two boxes of books for the new window display.

Max Davies, the owner of Chez Cuisine, had taken a while to grow on me, but it turned out that he had great taste in cookbooks. I'd promised him we'd do a new display with some titles he'd recommended. It had taken a bit of coaxing for me to convince him that we needed not only true cookbooks but also some other titles – like Ruth Reichl's *Save Me The Plums* – to round out the display. But his list of recommendations turned out to be stellar and diverse, and I was eager to get the books into the window for the afternoon.

Daniel hefted the boxes onto the display platform and gave me a quick hug before heading over to his garage. For the past couple of weeks, he'd spent the first couple of hours of Saturday morning here at the shop helping me with displays and shelving. He wasn't much of a reader, but he was *all in* for supporting the shop. Today, though, he had car repairs to manage, so I focused on my display and looked forward to seeing him later.

I had just put the final book – *Eat This Poem* by Nicole Gulotta – into the display when David pulled up. Mart and I helped him unload his car, and then he and I headed out for lunch at the new BBQ place that had just opened up at the end of Main Street. I was a sucker for a place with a cute name, so Piggle and Shake had won me over as soon as the sign went up.

The author and I had a lovely lunch, and I was thrilled to hear that he had more books coming in his renovation series. I knew his military thrillers were good, too, but I was much more a mystery girl myself.

After our meal, I pointed him in the direction of the co-op and gave him the address for the maritime museum before heading back to the shop for the afternoon. St. Marin's wasn't San Francisco in terms of entertainment, but in some ways, it was even better. At least here, everything was within easy walking distance of everything else. Plus, since I knew Cate would take good care of David at the co-op and then Lucas would do the same at the museum, I didn't worry that he might get bored or frustrated. They'd agreed to give him the behind-the-scenes tour and have him back to the shop by five so we could all get dinner before the reading.

On my way back, I needed to stop by Elle Heron's farm stand to pick up some fresh flowers for the café tables and a bouquet for the signing table, too. Elle, a white woman in her sixties with light-brown hair cut into a bob, had been supplying fresh flowers – all grown at her small farm outside of town – since we opened, and this time, she was giving us some of the most amazing tulips I'd ever seen. The bright reds and yellows and purples would add just the right color to the store, and I couldn't wait to see what she'd put together for the main arrangement.

I shed my sweater as I walked the two blocks up to her shop – No Label; Just Farm to Table – and took a swig from my water bottle before I walked in. The day had grown quite warm, and I had broken my first sweat of the year, which was cause for a small celebration that I'd begun a decade ago in my first "summer" on the west side of San Francisco. There, the warm days come in mid-fall, when the fog burns off completely and the temperature climbs into the high seventies, maybe even low eighties. On each of those days, I walked to the corner market and got an ice cream from the chest freezer by the front door. Always the same thing every day until the fog returned. Sadly, "summer" in San Francisco rarely lasted more than two weeks.

Now, I was going to keep up that tradition with a slight modification. After all, I couldn't eat ice cream every day it got to eighty here. I wouldn't have minded eating ice cream every day from April to September, but I figured my cholesterol might mind. So just the first day, I decided. A celebration of the warmth returning.

"Hey Elle." I shouted as I walked toward the cooler, hopeful that she was as down-to-earth in her ice cream selection as she was about everything else. I wanted my plain, classic ice cream sandwich something fierce, and I was not disappointed.

I slid open the top of the freezer, and as I leaned down and grabbed my sandwich, something caught my eye. I stood up and took a step back.

Then, I dropped my ice cream on the floor as I backed into a shelf of broccoli and cabbage seedlings and sent potting soil and tiny plants flying.

Beside the cooler lay the body of Huckabee Harris, his muck boots covered in mud and his face as white as the vanilla ice cream now leaking out of the wrapper at my feet.

Grab your copy...
vinci-books.com/entitledkill

About the Author

ACF Bookens lives at the edge of Virginia's Blue Ridge Mountains with her young son and three playful cats. When she's not writing, she cross-stitches, plays too much Roblox with her kid, and does historical research on enslaved communities in the area.